THE KISSING PART

KYLIE GILMORE

Here's to the magic of first love!

1

Owen

"No, I don't think it's about time I settled down."

I move up in line at Something's Brewing Café. This isn't the first time Aunt Hailey has asked me about love, commitment, all that BS, and it won't be the last. There's a reason I'm a die-hard bachelor. Anyway, she means well.

"When was the last time you met a nice woman?" she presses with a sunny smile, her pale blue eyes sparkling. She's in her fifties and looks much younger thanks to healthy living, as she says.

I wrap an arm around her and pull her in for a side hug. "It's good to see you too."

She gives me a playful shove. "Owen Campbell, such a charmer. Just keep an open heart, that's all I'm saying. You never know when you'll turn around and fall suddenly, madly in love."

"That's not how it went down with you and Uncle Josh." Their frenemy rivalry turned into all-out war back in the day. Much to Aunt Hailey's embarrassment, their story is an endless source of entertainment for both our family and the small town of Clover Park, Connecticut. Tough for the town's premier wedding planner. Her company is called Love

Junkies, which tells you all you need to know about her take on life.

She tosses her long strawberry blonde hair over one shoulder. "That's because he was a beast. It took time for him to show his true sweeter colors."

I put in my order for coffee and buy hers too. We step to the side to wait.

"Thanks for the coffee," she says. "Is Mackenzie seeing anyone?" That's her daughter.

I put my hands up. "Not touching that one." My cousin Mackenzie works with me in a small high-tech security company.

"She's just so secretive about her love life."

Gee, wonder why. Not only is Aunt Hailey a matchmaker by nature and a wedding planner, she runs a long-standing romance book club called the Happy Endings Book Club. Uncle Josh named his bar after it, Happy Endings. No, not that kind of happy ending. Ha.

Mackenzie doesn't believe in love. I know, ironic with her mom. Can't say I disagree with her. Love is for suckers.

I try to sound reassuring. "I'm sure if there was anything serious, Mackenzie would bring him home to meet the family."

Aunt Hailey purses her lips. "I just worry she takes the warrior part too seriously. She has more armor around her heart than you do. I don't think she's ever been in love."

Aunt Hailey has called herself a warrior princess for as long as I can remember, and she calls Uncle Josh a warrior beast. Mackenzie says she's no dainty princess, she's a badass warrior queen. I'll say this for her, she doesn't take shit from anyone. I once witnessed her and my sister, Harper, have a knockdown fight when they were little girls with legit punches and kicks over who got to play with Harper's doll's Corvette. Harper insisted it was hers, so she should get it, and Mackenzie said the guest gets to play with what they want. Forget about taking turns. Probably didn't help that Mackenzie, a year younger and smaller, had been trained in self-defense since she could walk. Her dad, Uncle Josh, was a paratrooper in the Army, skilled in hand-to-hand combat, and wanted his three kids to have self-defense skills.

"Owen!" the barista calls.

I head over to the counter. "Thanks."

I take the coffee tray and hand Aunt Hailey her coffee.

She goes up on tiptoe to kiss me on the cheek. "I'll see you on Saturday night for the double graduation slash grandparents' anniversary party."

"See you then." My family's so big—Dad was one of six with honorary brothers too—that there's always some occasion to celebrate. This time it's Grandpop Joe and Grandmom Brandy's anniversary, as well as my brother and cousin's college graduation party. It helps that Uncle Josh owns the Happy Endings bar to host all our family events. It's not just a bar. There's a full restaurant and a back room with pool tables, a jukebox, and a dance floor.

I jog upstairs to our office and set the coffee tray on the kitchen table.

"Oh, good, you're here," Mackenzie calls from the next room.

"Yeah," I say, distracted by a text on my phone.

Mom: *I need to see you right away. Stop by the Summerdale library. We're wrapping up filming.*

A jolt of adrenaline fires through me. It's the "right away." Mom is Claire Jordan, a world-famous actor, producer, and director. I have a love-hate relationship with show business because of what it does to people, and how it can make famous people unsafe. Mom's had more than her share of stalkers and overzealous fans. When I was a kid, she had a full-time bodyguard, Frank, who lived in our guesthouse and oversaw her security as well as ours. He's retired now. His son, Frankie, took over where he left off.

Me: *Be there in fifteen.*

I pull my key fob from my jeans pocket and bolt to the door, yelling over my shoulder, "I'll text you later."

"What about our meeting?" Mackenzie asks.

I jog downstairs and take the door to the parking lot in back.

Mom's been taking more chances with public outings than I'd like. She used to be much more careful. She claims she's stalker-free, but you never know when a new one will pop up. Her old movies play regularly on TV. She's doing more behind-the-camera work now. Still. Just recently she played the MILF next door in a limited series on one of the streamers. I know. It's my *mom*. She's the one who called it the MILF next door.

Her appeal puts her at risk, and that's where I come in. Bodyguard Frank taught me everything I know about krav maga—street fighting—as well as weapons work with knives, rope, and guns. I don't carry weapons, but I like knowing how to use them. I could take them away from an opponent if needed. Harper and my brother, Rafael, could've learned self-defense too, but they had no interest. We've been the target of paparazzi since birth. As the oldest, I looked out for them.

I get into my black Mustang and peel out of the lot. Frankie should be with her. She's fine. It's probably nothing. Then why did she say right away?

I turn onto Main Street, take the first right onto Route 15, and floor it.

~

Shayla

I peer between the books on the shelf to whisper, "It's a silent night."

A red-haired woman looks back at me. "Good night for a hunt." She slips me a leather-bound book, but when I reach for it, she doesn't let go. "You have until midnight."

I nod and take the book, browsing other books for a few moments before slipping away. When I walk into the open area of the library, she's gone.

"Cut," the director, Levi Appleton, says. "Shayla, perfect

amount of tension. Josie, let's try it again with the alternate version of your line."

Not hard to be tense when you're about to see the only man you've ever loved for the first time in nine years. At least I hope so. His mom, Claire, asked him to come here ASAP. She didn't say it was on my behalf. He might not have come.

My costar, Josie Abbott, flashes a bright smile and says the alternate line, "Brady isn't what he seems. Clock's ticking. Midnight."

I go back into position behind the shelf. We're in the second-floor loft area of the Summerdale library in a pretty country area of New York. Tomorrow we move to New York City for the final six weeks of filming.

I've been a working actor since I was seven years old. Once I finally shed the child-star persona by playing an angsty heroine in a dark fantasy, the majority of my roles were in the same vein. This role is different. I get to be the hero in a military action romance based on Audrey Robinson's book *Breakdown*. I'm part of a secret unit called into action to work with a handsome civilian who may have ties to organized crime. For once I get to be a stoic badass instead of bawling my eyes out.

We run through the scene a second time and wait for Levi's reaction.

"Cut!" he says cheerfully. "That's a wrap for the scene. Good work, everyone. Let's pack up."

The crew starts to pack away equipment, and the actors make their way to the main level, where the author and her family are watching. I hold back, looking for Owen. When I last saw him, he was seventeen, wiry with muscle and athletic. Claire has kept me updated with family pictures over the years. He has a dark beard now that suits him, and he's filled out in the shoulders and chest, all of him muscular looking.

Claire walks over and gives me a reassuring smile. "Good work today. How're you feeling?" The tension in my shoulders drops. She's like a mom to me. My own toxic mom, who was also my manager, nearly broke me. I became an emancipated minor at sixteen, dove into the Hollywood party scene, and started making headlines for all the wrong reasons. Claire had worked with me when I was eight years old, saw what was going on, and invited me to come live with her family in Connecticut for the summer.

She helped me put my life back together, taught me how to navigate the industry as an adult, how to handle being put on a pedestal by the press and the public, and also how to handle being knocked off that pedestal with grace. In short, she taught me to be grounded. My work is not me. I'm a worthy person in my own right with many varied interests, like interior design, knitting, and her son. Yeah. I never got over Owen.

We fell in love, and everything was *perfect*. Until it wasn't.

"I'm nervous," I admit. "What if he doesn't want to see me?"

She smooths my blond hair back and kisses my temple. "He has a protective streak a mile wide. The minute he hears about your stalker, he's going to check in with you."

Yup, that's right. I'm officially an A-list star. I've got a stalker. His name is Matt Boone, thirty, divorced, and obsessed with my former role as a runaway teen who turns to prostitution to survive. I used to have a bodyguard, but I couldn't relax around him. Was it the fact that he never took his sunglasses off? I don't know. There was a vibe that never sat right with me, so when he quit for another gig, I was relieved. And then I thought of Owen, hoping it was an opportunity to see if there was anything there between us after all these years. He runs a security firm.

Will he still be interested in me now that I'm a successful actor? I hope he'd be proud of what I've made of myself. On the other hand, it was show business that took me away from him in the first place. A choice I made that I've had to live with. I don't regret choosing to leave Connecticut for my big-break movie, but I often wondered over the years, what if I'd stayed? Would we still be together today?

I blow out a shaky breath. Maybe he's moved on and forgotten all about me. This may not have been my best plan. Rejection after all my hopeful buildup over the years would be devastating. I always thought the reason no relationship worked out for me after Owen was because I was meant to be with him. It was just a matter of timing.

I'm in a good place now. If he—okay, cool it. I need to bring my expectations down. If I can make amends for the past, and we become friendly again, I'm calling it a win. Anything more is a bonus.

Please let him be happy to see me.

Anyway, I do have a temporary bodyguard to keep me safe. Since I've been filming in New York, Claire's bodyguard, Frankie, has been working double duty for the two of us.

She links her arm through mine. "Let's go chat with everyone while we wait."

I follow her to the lobby, where the author, Audrey, is surrounded by friends. This production has been a lot of Summerdale people, along with Claire's friends from nearby Clover Park. I stand near Claire while the ladies, most of them in their forties and fifties, talk excitedly about the movie. It's nearly all women here. I won't meet the male lead until we start filming in the city. Claire's the producer of this film. She's known for women-forward movies with a large proportion of women staff. It's unusual to have a male director on one of her films, but Levi is a friend of actor Harper Ellis, also in the movie. She highly recommended him. Levi and Harper grew up together in Summerdale.

He's here.

Sweat breaks out on my forehead. Where's that makeup artist when I need her? I discreetly wipe away sweat as I watch Owen approach. The pictures didn't do him justice. He moves with the confidence of a man who knows his place in this world. Dark hair, dark eyes, and a trimmed dark beard that makes him look slightly dangerous. His white T-shirt stretches across wide shoulders and bulging biceps, and his faded jeans show off strong thighs. My pulse spikes. I underestimated what it would do to me, seeing him in person again. I can still hear his husky voice whispering in my ear. That night. That beautiful disaster of a night.

He's intercepted by Audrey's petite teenaged twin girls, who ask him questions. He nods at them, looking around and then zeroing in on his mom.

Claire turns to him. "Owen, you're here." She gives him a hug. He returns it, glancing sideways at the twin girls who followed him. They look like they're crushing hard. I don't blame them. He's a stunner.

I wipe clammy hands on my black trousers. What should I say? *Hi, it's been a long time.* Or maybe more upbeat. *Hey, Owen, good to see you again. Will you help me out with my stalker situation and also forgive me and give me a second chance?*

Hmm…stalker doesn't exactly scream upbeat.

Gah! Why am I so nervous? We've both grown up enough to move past what happened. Right? Right?!

I can't seem to get a deep breath. This was a bad idea.

"You said you had to see me right away," Owen says to Claire. He looks around. "Where's Frankie?"

"He's waiting right outside," Claire says. "Anyway, this is Harper's hometown. She said we don't have to worry about security here. It's a closed set, and everyone we're working with is a close friend."

Owen nods and then stiffens as he suddenly notices me.

I swallow hard. Words fail me. I consider waving, but I can't seem to move my frozen limbs.

He clenches his jaw. "If this has something to do with *her*, then I pass."

Clearly he didn't move past what happened between us. We were so young. What was I supposed to do?

I step closer, wanting him to understand. Where to start?

He crosses his arms over his chest, looking like a fortress forever closed off to me. Claire jumps in to smooth things over.

"Just listen," she says to Owen. "Shay could use your company's help."

He keeps his mouth clamped shut.

"Are you a bodyguard?" one of the twin girls asks Owen.

He ignores her in favor of staring me down. I don't look away. I know this man, at least I did. He has a good heart, a warm and loving nature. I've never met another man like him.

Claire gives my hand a squeeze before sending a significant look to the twin girls' dad. He guides them away while they whisper fiercely to each other.

"Shayla has a stalker who's determined to get to her," Claire says.

Owen's arms drop to his sides, his voice gruff as his dark eyes meet mine. "Tell me everything."

He cares. My limbs feel lighter, a ray of hope shining through. It's a start.

2

———

Owen

Shayla's in trouble. My fingers itch with the need to haul her into my arms and keep her there safe. I don't dare touch her. Instead, I incline my head for her to follow me.

We reach the front desk of the closed library.

"It's good to see you again, Owen," she says with a small smile.

My gut tightens as memories flood me. She was a curvy blonde-haired, blue-eyed fantasy at sixteen. Now she's impossibly sexy, and I'm doing my damnedest to stay focused on her eyes. Not her luscious lips, her generous curves, or the sweet line of her neck, where I loved to nuzzle and breathe her in.

She was friends with my sister Harper first. Whenever I went by them, Shayla would always call me by name with just a hint of flirt behind it, "Hi, Owen," "Nice to see you, Owen," "Don't be a stranger, Owen." I started overusing her name, and the next thing you know, we're meeting in the loft over the detached garage.

I fell *hard*.

Which has no relevance today. I don't care how much I'm attracted to her. Dammit. Can my brain and body please get on the same page? I know better.

Maybe *she's* attracted to *me*, and that's the tension I'm feeling between us. Or maybe I'm just stressed by the fact that Mom acted like she had a freaking emergency only to spring Shayla on me.

I keep my voice cool, calm, and professional. "Wish it were under better circumstances for you."

Her gaze tracks from my eyes to my cheek and jaw and then back. "Yeah."

"So, what's his profile, what's he done so far, and what have you done to protect yourself?" Stalkers are nearly always male.

She glances around. "Can we go somewhere more private? I don't like sharing all the dirt in public."

The library is closed, but cast and crew still mill about. I understand the need for discretion.

"We could talk outside," I say.

"I don't want to chance someone overhearing. People are still coming and going. How about my car? I could ask the driver to step out."

I consider that. The thing about a car is the close proximity. It's one thing to stay cool when there's space between us. No space equals a temptation I don't even want to consider. And what if she cries because of the stalker situation? I'll practically be required to hold her, one thing will lead to another, and that spells disaster.

"How about we meet up at Mom's house?" No chance of privacy there. Mom will be wanting to know all. She's super protective of Shayla, which is probably why she called me to deal with this problem.

"Are you afraid to be alone with me in a car?" she teases.

"No. It's just too confining. I need to spread out to think."

"Uh-huh."

I cross my arms, working on looking tough. I'm not going to get sucked in by her flirty charm. "So what about Mom's house?"

"I'm staying at a hotel in the city."

"Why wouldn't you stay with Mom? Her place is wired

top to bottom for security, and Frankie lives in the guesthouse."

"I was there for a few days, but my things were moved to the hotel today since filming starts in the city tomorrow."

"I'm not trekking all the way to the city to talk." Translation: we will not be alone in a hotel room.

"Okay, so pick a place where you can spread out and think."

I give her side-eye, not appreciating her teasing when I'm doing her a *favor* coming up with a security plan. "Little respect here, Miss Big-Time Movie Star."

Her lips curve up, her eyes dancing with amusement. "Mucho respect, Mr. Security Expert."

I frown. "This is serious business."

She steps closer, her voice soft. "That's why I wanted you."

My body flushes with heat. Not because I'm turned on. No way. It's because she's showing the respect I deserve. It's pride that makes me warmer because I'm good at my job.

I consider the Happy Endings bar as a meeting place, my home territory, but decide she'll attract too much attention. "We can meet in my office in Clover Park." I hand her my phone. "Put your number in. I'll text you the address. You can drive over with your bodyguard." I look around for her guard. "Where is he?"

"Is your office on Main Street?" she asks as she types her number in my phone. "I remember Clover Park well, and all the family get-togethers with your cousins at Happy Endings, sometimes at the park. God, I have such fond memories of that town." She hands me back my phone.

"Yeah, it's on Main Street. Where's your guard?"

"I've been using Frankie while I'm here."

"Well, I know he's not going into the city with you, unless Mom's joining you there."

"How're Cooper and Finn? I already know how Mackenzie's doing since we've..." She trails off.

A tension vibrates between us and not the sexy kind. She

kept in touch with my cousin Mackenzie, Mom, and my sister, Harper, but not me. Not gonna lie, that cut deep.

I back up a step. "You know what? If you need my company to set up security, you can get in touch with Mackenzie. She sets up all new clients anyway. Mom thought of me first because she knows I understand the whole famous-person thing. I'm sure Mackenzie will understand too."

She grabs my arm. "Wait. It's you I want."

My heart lurches. God, how much I longed to hear those words back then. A rush of sensation washes over my arm as she burrows her hand under my T-shirt sleeve, an old habit of hers. Part of me wants to push her hand away; part of me likes it too much.

She looks up at me, her blue eyes pleading and so damn vulnerable I have to fight the urge to go caveman and carry her out of here to the safety of my place. "My bodyguard got another gig and quit. Your mom said I could borrow Frankie until I found a new one."

I look pointedly at her hand until she removes it. "I'm not a bodyguard. I can secure your hotel room, your tech, and that's it."

"But you trained with Frankie's dad."

"That's not what I do. I'm going to get Frankie. Maybe he knows someone."

I walk out the side door, where I can see Frankie with Mom and her friends. I relax a little when I don't hear Shayla's footsteps behind me.

"Hey, Frankie." I give him a one-armed hug. He's four years older than me and like a brother. He's half Hawaiian, half Italian, a hulk of a man with a shaved head and an easy smile. His Hawaiian dad only found out about him when Frankie's mom died in a car accident when Frankie was ten. We used to spar together after his dad trained us both in krav maga. Fun times.

"Bro, your mom's doing fine."

I check in with him regularly on her security situation. So sue me if I'm protective. It's for a legit reason.

"Good. I was wondering if you might know someone to be Shayla's shadow in the city."

"Isn't that what you're here for? That's what your mom said, and I know you always come through for her."

She did? No one told me.

I frown. "You must know someone."

"Everyone I know is gainfully employed and not in the bodyguard business. You think I belong to a union? I'm part of the Claire Jordan family, and I'm not going anywhere. No sweeter gig. She still makes me and Dad the best grilled cheese sandwiches. And she regularly invites the—" cough "—nicest women to go horseback riding with us. I never knew how many women love riding. Must be the rocking motion, you know?"

Nice. Mom's been keeping Frankie in grilled cheese and beautiful women who ride. Me she calls to deal with stalkers.

I catch Mom's eye, and she joins us.

"Owen, please do this for her," she says. "Shayla feels safe with you. It's just a temporary thing until we can find someone new for her."

"I'm busy with other clients. I have a big job that could come through any moment in DC and—"

"That's wonderful, honey!" she says. "In the meantime, could you do what you do best? You'll be paid of course."

I scowl. "I wouldn't take her money if I were starving in the street. I can't believe you're putting me in this position."

An icy feminine voice calls out behind me, "Don't worry about it, Owen. I'll be just fine. So good to see you again."

I whirl. "Shay, I—"

She darts into the library.

"Don't just stand there looking guilty," Mom says. "Go after her."

I exhale sharply and walk toward the door.

"The chase is on...at a snail's pace," Frankie says with a laugh.

"Shut up," I say over my shoulder just before I step inside.

I don't see her. My heart pounds. She can't afford to sulk alone somewhere when she's got a stalker after her. I didn't even find out who it is or what he looks like.

I weave through the shelves on the lower level, peer into the children's room, and dash to the loft area, nearly knocking over a guy carrying a boom mike out. She couldn't have just disappeared.

I check the bathrooms and even the back room behind the counter. No Shayla.

I walk up to a woman wheeling a camera out the double front doors. "Have you seen Shayla?"

"Yeah, she went to her car. I think she's heading back to the city."

"Thanks."

I should've thought of that. She went in one door and out the other. I rush to the parking lot and spot a black Mercedes with tinted windows parked nearby. The car's running, so I knock on the driver's side window to keep them here.

The window powers down, and a man in his sixties with salt-and-pepper hair stares at me. "Who are you?"

"I'm Shayla's friend. Claire Jordan's son Owen."

"I thought you looked familiar. I remember pictures from when you lost your two front teeth." Paparazzi strike again.

"I need to speak to her." I shift to the back window and knock on it.

The window powers down. Shayla lifts her chin in a way that says she's digging her heels in. "I don't need your help."

"Yes, you do. Go to my office, and we'll hammer out the details."

"No."

"No?"

"No."

"So you no longer have a stalker desperate to get to you while you stay alone in a hotel room in a city of more than a million people who'd recognize you anywhere?"

"The hotel has a doorman and cameras in the lobby."

I take a deep breath. "I'm not letting you put yourself at risk."

"Why?"

"Because…you're you."

Her expression softens. "Maybe we could catch up."

"We need a security plan. Not—"

The window slowly closes. "I'll meet you there."

I stare at my own reflection in the tinted glass. How did I end up insisting on helping when I wanted nothing to do with her?

Shayla

"What's your plan for tonight?" Owen asks.

We're standing in the meeting room of his office, which is obviously a living room in a one-bedroom apartment. They've done little to make it more office-like. Framed arty black-and-white photos hang on the walls, most likely Mackenzie's picks. A utilitarian faux-wood table and black swivel chairs dominate the living room space. I peek into the bedroom, which has a long wraparound workspace against the walls and three chairs. Guess that's command central.

"My plan is to meet with you, and then go back to my hotel," I say before wandering back to the kitchen area. At least this is a cozier space with warm wood cabinets, a farmhouse sink, and a round table with chairs. I'm a fan of good interior design. If I weren't an actor, I might've become an interior designer.

Owen follows me in. "I meant your security plan for tonight. Is Frankie meeting up with you later?"

"If I ask him to. I'm hungry. Are you hungry?" I open the refrigerator, which is stocked with fresh fruit and vegetables, as well as homemade salad dressing, mixed nuts, and cheese. Thank you, Mackenzie. Her mom always emphasized the importance of eating healthy to feel and look good, and she took that to heart. I like to eat the same way, and actually, I have to. If I gain weight, it means wardrobe changes and less marketability. Sad but true for the industry.

I pull out raspberries, cheese, and the mixed greens.

"Help yourself," Owen says with a hint of sarcasm.

"Thank you." I set the food on the counter and open a cabinet, searching for a plate. "I'm used to making myself at home in a variety of places. Comes with the territory. New locations for every project."

"We have chamomile tea." His deep voice sounds by my ear. Goosebumps rise on my arms in contrast to the heat of his body at my back. He remembered I like chamomile tea at night.

He reaches over my head to get a wooden box.

I turn, nearly in his arms.

His gaze heats as our eyes meet up close. "Here." As soon as I take the box, he retreats to the kitchen table.

"Thanks." I pull out a tea bag and glance over my shoulder to where he's sitting at the table, long legs stretched out and crossed at the ankles. I have the sudden urge to curl up in his lap, the only place I've ever felt like the world couldn't touch me. He's one of those rare breeds of men who'll hold you with no further agenda. Dare I say he was a cuddler? But that was seventeen-year-old Owen. He might not be that person anymore.

I set the tea kettle to boil and assemble my dinner on a plate. I'm sure this is Mackenzie's box of teas. I'm getting together with her and Harper on Saturday in the city. I can't wait. It's been too long. They came out to visit me in LA three years ago, and that was the last time I saw them.

A short while later, I join him at the table with my late dinner.

"So tell me about your stalker," he says.

I fill him in as I eat. He listens carefully, asking lots of questions on the various run-ins I've had with Matt.

"So basically he's hoping he can use you as a prostitute just like in the movie," Owen concludes.

"That's right. He often refers to the fact that he can afford me."

"I assume you have a restraining order."

"Yes. He still managed to break into my house in LA and somehow found me at a retreat in Belize."

He blows out a breath. "He must have money to afford traveling. Have you seen him in New York?"

I take a sip of tea. "Not yet, but I have a feeling he'll show up in the city. Much easier to blend with the crowd."

"What's your situation at the hotel?"

"I've got the penthouse suite. Two bedrooms with a terrace. Claire said Frankie could take the room below mine by the private elevator to monitor anyone who might approach."

He exhales sharply. "Mom's had her share of stalkers over the years. She didn't tell us all the details, but I looked it up online. She once found a guy naked in her bed."

"She told me."

He shakes his head. "It's sick that just because you appear on a screen, people think they have a right to you."

"Part of the territory. I just want to feel safe again." I hesitate, tempted to ask him to move in with me for the six weeks I'm here, knowing it's never going to happen. "Are you still a paparazzi favorite?"

"They've sort of lost interest in me and my siblings since we grew up. Besides, there's bigger, younger stars than Mom now to follow."

"Not bigger, just younger. She's still got a long career ahead of her, one of those rare female actors who keep getting roles their whole lives. She's the epitome of aging gracefully. I aspire to do the same."

"You're twenty-five. Are you telling me you seriously think about aging gracefully?"

"Hello? It's part of the business. Women age out of roles quickly. They always want the next pretty young thing."

"That's—never mind. Back to your security needs."

"No, wait. What were you going to say?"

He taps the table. "Let's stay on track. Tomorrow I'll send Nathan to scope out your suite, and then we'll figure out the best way to secure it."

"Do you think it's horrible that women age out quickly? That maybe I'm already past my prime?"

He leans forward. "How can you even think that? I was going to say that's not something you need to worry about."

I hide a smile behind my mug of tea. Hope dances in my heart. "Owen, I really appreciate you taking this on. I know you're busy."

"Of course. So, like I said, Nathan will scope out the place with you tomorrow. What time is good for you?"

"I want *you*."

He looks just past my shoulder. "Nathan knows the ropes."

"Nathan tossed me and Harper in the pool."

He straightens and looks me in the eye. "That was years ago. He was just horsing around. Don't you know when a guy throws you into the pool, it means he likes you?"

"He threw both of us. Besides, he knew I was with you." *Oops.* I wasn't planning on touching on our past so soon. "He and Harper fought like cats and dogs. He was just being a jerk."

He scrubs a hand over his beard. "Once we've added security to your place, we'll need to find a bodyguard to stay with you. If we find someone you're comfortable with, they could take one of the bedrooms. That's better than a floor below. From what you describe, it sounds like Matt's getting bolder in his attempts to get to you."

"Whoever I hire, I'd have to trust them with my life."

"Of course."

"And they need to pass the vibe check. The last guy, something felt off. I guess it was lucky he got a better gig and quit. I never felt comfortable with him."

"Naturally. A vibe," he says drily.

"And of course I'd pay them triple their going rate

because they would absolutely be worth having peace of mind. That would be helpful to any small security firm."

Our gazes collide as he suddenly realizes I'm talking about him.

"I don't want your money," he says.

"I'd only be paying what my peace of mind is worth."

"Frankie can live with you. And I'll tell Mom to ask Frank to go out with her."

"Frank's old."

"He's in his sixties, but he's still fit. He taught me everything I know about street fighting and weapons."

"Did he teach Nathan the same thing?"

"No."

"You see why it has to be you?"

"Shay—"

"Please, Owen. The moment my guard quit, I thought of you. Your mom told me about your company. I knew it was the perfect solution."

I hold my breath.

"I'm not a bodyguard," he finally says. "I don't even have a permit to carry a gun."

"That's easily remedied."

"I already have a job."

"You know why you're better than a bodyguard? I can relax around you, which will do wonders for my state of mind. Mental health is important, you know. Just as important as physical health, well, maybe not exactly as important, but pretty close—"

"I'll find you someone else." He stands. "We should go. I'll fill the team in on what you told me and get back to you tomorrow."

My gut does a slow roll. Here I was hoping this was going to be a fresh beginning for us when Owen wants nothing to do with me.

3

The next morning I go to our rescheduled office meeting with my own agenda and coffee to sweeten the deal. Half the time we work from home or we're out on a job, but today we managed to get the three of us together.

"Hey, boss," Nathan says as I walk in.

"Hey, boss," I reply. "Nice try on growing a beard."

He rubs his dark stubbled jaw. "Give it time. Soon I'll have your level of beard, and I'll finally get a break from women throwing themselves at me."

"Ha-ha." Nathan is abnormally good looking with his brown hair in an expensive neat cut, blue eyes, and the kind of cheekbones and jaw you see in ads. He was a model starting in his teens through college. He's nobody's wingman, but I keep him around because he's loyal. He was my next-door neighbor growing up in a rural area of Connecticut, where kids were few and far between. I trust him with my life.

"The boss queen has arrived," Mackenzie says as she strides in with her satchel. Her long wavy brown hair is up in a messy bun. Unlike Aunt Hailey's penchant for designer dresses and lots of pink, Mackenzie favors T-shirts, jeans, and sneakers. And never pink. I'd say it's a rebellion against her mom, but they're close. As long as Aunt Hailey doesn't probe about Mackenzie's love life.

The three of us are equal partners in Brooks Campbell Security. Nathan is Nathan Brooks. His name is first purely for alphabetical reasons. Oh, and he invested the most. And the Campbell is for me, Owen Campbell, and my cousin Mackenzie Campbell. Nathan and I work on location with clients while Mackenzie does marketing and accounting. And basically runs the company.

Mackenzie settles at the meeting table and efficiently takes out her laptop and papers.

I set the coffee down and hand my cousin hers. "Saw your mom downstairs at the café yesterday."

Mackenzie raises her blue eyes to mine. "Please tell me she didn't bug you about your love life."

"Well, then it wouldn't be Aunt Hailey, would it? How else could she stay in business so long in small-town Clover Park? She's practically required to arrange couples to walk down the aisle."

Mackenzie smiles as she boots up her laptop. "Well, she is a master networker. I'm always amazed at how far her reach is." She stops smiling. "She didn't ask about *my* love life, did she? Never mind. Don't tell me."

I grin. "I told her about your latest walk of shame, and she nearly fainted."

Nathan chuckles and takes his coffee. "I'm overdue for my walk of shame."

"No shame in enjoying consensual fun," Mackenzie replies easily as she taps her keyboard. "So, let's get down to business. I've got lots to do today. Our virtual assistant deserves a raise. Sutton's been with us three months and exceeded expectations."

"How does Sutton manage to be sunshine all the time from a cold place like Minnesota?" Nathan asks.

"It's not cold all the time," I say.

"Are we in agreement?" Mackenzie asks. "I'd like to bump her up ten dollars an hour and revisit it again in six months. We don't want to lose the first good assistant we've hired."

"Agreed," Nathan and I say at the same time.

"Good, moving on," Mackenzie says, turning her laptop screen toward us. "Projected revenue for next quarter and year-end." She has an accounting degree and can basically do anything.

I pull the laptop closer. "Year-end is looking weak."

Nathan sips his coffee. "We should be going up year after year, not losing ground."

"We've got a good foothold with tech companies and pharma," Mackenzie says. "It's time to reach another industry. Our government contract is looking promising. High security clearance, which means high profile for us. Only thing is, they delayed choosing a contractor until after the Fourth of July holiday. And they want someone in DC for at least eight weeks right after that."

"I can't," Nathan says. "I promised the fam I'd meet them in Martha's Vineyard for the Fourth and the two weeks after. It's on the calendar."

I ball up a napkin and throw it at him. "I can do it. How close are we to getting it? Fifty percent chance? Seventy-five?"

Mackenzie purses her lips, looking just like her mom. Funny how thinking expressions can be inherited. "Seventy-five. I feel good about this one. I sent over our latest work with Iotech's cancer vaccine security. That was a good one with the techie alarm systems, as well as cyber security."

Nathan and I can do all the tech needed for our clients, even though neither of us has a degree in computer science. He has a degree in business, and mine is in mechanical engineering. After six months at an engineering firm, I went out on my own, partnering up with these two. Dad is a genius with computers and taught me everything I know. He founded Dat Cloud to compress data at a time when it was overwhelming systems. He sold it for a huge profit. Nathan was over at the house so much he picked up the computer stuff too. We used to do a lot of online gaming and hacked our way into stuff we had no business messing with just to see if we could. Hey, the best hackers make for the best cyber-security experts.

"Anything you two would like to add?" Mackenzie asks.

"Shayla Adler wants to hire us for help with a stalker situation," I say in my professional voice as if she has zero effect on me. Which she doesn't.

"She told me," Mackenzie says.

I stare at her. "When?" *And why did Shayla come to me if she could just as easily have gone to Mackenzie?*

Is Shayla hoping to start something with me?

My shoulders tense. No way I'm going down that road again with her.

"Last night," Mackenzie says. "I think you should do it."

I shake my head. "Nathan should take this one for security setup, and then I want you to find her a bodyguard. I'm out."

"Owen, our year-end figures are looking dismal," Mackenzie says. "Shayla will pay big bucks, and she specifically wants you. This could be an 'in' with a new industry. Think of all the high-tech equipment the movie industry needs to keep safe, not to mention the intellectual property and their stars."

"I already have an insider connection with Mom," I say, though I would never use it. Dad hammered it into our brains that we needed to make our own way in the world. No special treatment. He taught me computer stuff, but he expected me to handle career stuff solo. Besides, I *want* to make my own way in the world.

I cross my arms. "My schedule's full."

Mackenzie smiles. "I've already rearranged a few things on your schedule. Nathan and I will pick up the slack so you can dedicate two weeks to the Shayla job."

I clench my jaw. I either have to deal with Shayla or let down my partners, knowing we could really use the business.

Nathan jerks his chin at me. "You can handle being near the most beautiful woman in the world for two weeks, right?"

I give him the finger. He knows what went down between me and Shayla.

"Do it for Brooks Campbell Security," Nathan says. "Bottom line, we can't afford to turn away lucrative jobs."

"Do it for a woman who's scared to go to work, scared to go anywhere," Mackenzie says.

My Achilles' heel. A woman in need of protection. Not just any woman. The one who snuck into my heart and then blew it up.

I scrub a hand over my face. "Fine. Two weeks, but I'm not living with her. I'm staying in the room below her."

Mackenzie's brows shoot up. "Who said anything about living together?"

"I told her it was best if her bodyguard took the extra bedroom for her safety." I feel like an ass recommending something I have no intention of doing. But how the hell can I resist temptation living in the same hotel suite for two weeks?

"Then I suppose that's on your conscience," Mackenzie says. "I know it's not easy for you, but look at it this way, after all these years, you can finally move on."

I bristle. "I have moved on. In fact, it's no problem at all to take the extra bedroom."

"Big words, man," Nathan says. "Sure you can handle it?"

"I'm a professional," I snarl.

Mackenzie nods once. "Right. Anything else on the agenda for today?"

If I'm going to do a job, I'm going to do it right. Obviously I'm over her. I've had girlfriends. Plenty. And I've seen Shayla with plenty of actors, models, and rock stars in pictures plastered everywhere. I'm not looking for them, believe me.

Nathan leans back in his chair. "We should have an office party to celebrate three years of being in business together."

"It was three years in January," Mackenzie says.

"Yeah, but I just thought about it now," Nathan says. "Besides, the weather's better in May. We could have it at my place."

"Does this have anything to do with Harper being back in

town?" I ask. My younger sister has a love-hate relationship with Nathan. As in, she loves to hate him, and he's baffled by it. I don't understand it either. They were close when we were kids.

"No," Nathan says defensively. "Can't a guy celebrate his company's success? What's she got against me anyhow?" He takes a casual sip of coffee, but his eyes are glued to mine.

"I don't know. Ask her," I say like I always do.

He frowns. "She always says it's nothing, but she's still prickly around me."

Mackenzie types away on her laptop, working again. "We're in the black for now, but we're still in the growing stages. I wouldn't say we're a success yet, Nathan."

"In the black is a success," I say.

Our phones alert us to new emails.

Mackenzie keeps typing as she speaks. "Just emailed you both a summary of the DC job. Let me know if we need to tweak anything. If you want to have an office party, I could ask Dad to reserve the back room for us at Happy Endings. It's more centrally located than Nathan's place high up the mountain in Eastman. Plus, no cleanup for us."

Nathan considers this. "But we always meet at Happy Endings."

"Because it's awesome," she says, clicking on her laptop. "There. Just gave Sutton a raise. I have a feeling she'll be a vital member of our team. You know, next meeting we should have her call in. We're so used to doing things ourselves that we forget we have this great resource." She looks up from the laptop and sips her coffee for the first time. "Too bad she lives so far away. She'd be fun to hang with."

"Mackenzie's making friends," Nathan singsongs.

"I like her," she says. "Are we good to book Happy Endings over the long Memorial day weekend, Saturday night? Dad and Cooper have been talking about a special summer menu. I'll invite our friends and clients with a plus one. We could make some good contacts for future business. You never know where you'll meet the next big client."

"Yeah, let's do it," Nathan says. "Let me see the RSVP list when you get it."

"Shayla," Mackenzie says to me, shooing me out the door.

I hold two fingers up. *Two weeks. That's it.*

I stand and grab my coffee.

She turns to Nathan. "Why do you need to see the RSVP list? Hoping for a certain someone?"

"No."

Mackenzie takes pity on him. "You'll see her at the double graduation slash anniversary party this weekend."

"See who?" Nathan asks innocently.

Mackenzie rolls her eyes. "You've been warned."

"Think you can handle Harper this time around?" I tease.

"Go see your long-lost love," he says blandly.

"This is a job," I bite out. "I'm doing this for the company."

"Right," Nathan says.

"Thank you!" Mackenzie carols.

As I drive to the city, my mind whirls with thoughts of Shayla. She crashed into my life once again, and just like the first time, I don't know whether I'm coming or going. Somehow I agreed to live with her because of course I will. My conscience couldn't take it if anything happened to her. Am I crazy?

I blame Mackenzie for bringing the business into it, saying we need this job, and that Shayla specifically wanted me.

She wanted me. Only me.

Just before I left, I texted Shayla that I'd be taking the job for two weeks. I expected an enthusiastic response. What I got was: *ok.*

Really? Just ok? Guess this is no big deal to her, which is fine. No messy entanglements.

Is Shayla safe at work? Did Frankie go with her? Did he stick around last night?

I stop at a red light and debate texting Frankie. No, it's fine. Of course Shayla wouldn't leave herself vulnerable in the city.

Guilt stabs at me. I should've gone with her last night.

Shayla looked so-o-o damn good. It was like no time passed at all when she looked into my eyes. She's not one of those actors who use plastic surgery to enhance their looks. She's got the same face, same luscious lips, and bright blue eyes, fresh-faced like sunshine. I inwardly groan. *Stop thinking about Shayla. No good can come of this.*

I've got to get out of this deal. Two weeks is way too long. Why would I want money from the business that stole her away from me? The memories come flooding back.

4

———

Nine years ago…

Shayla stands on the end of the diving board in her sexy yellow bikini and blows me a kiss. My heart thumps harder. I don't dare catch the kiss with my younger sister by a year and a half, Harper, here as a witness, but I can't help my grin.

Shayla dives smoothly into the deep end with barely a splash. She's the most beautiful girl I've ever met. Smart too. She reads Russian literature for fun. I can't believe my luck that Mom invited her to spend the summer with us in Connecticut. Even though she's only sixteen, she has her own house in LA because she's legally an emancipated minor. That means she declared herself independent from her mom. Her dad died long ago. Shayla's an actor like Mom. The only rule for her to stay with us is no alcohol and no drugs, which is fine. We don't need that shit to have fun.

She pops out of the water by me and beams. "Hey, *you*."

"Hey, *you*," I say warmly. My whole body feels warm whenever she's near.

"Cannonball!" Harper shouts right before she soaks us.

"Harper!" Shayla yells.

As soon as Harper pops up, I splash her. She sputters and splashes me back. Harper's always getting between me and

Shayla. Okay, so they were friends first. They're both sixteen. I'm seventeen. But Harper knows Shayla and I have a thing now. Everyone knows. It's cool with my parents. Though Mom warned me that Shayla will likely be leaving if she gets another gig, and Dad warned me not to have sex with her because Shayla's working on being more her authentic self, and sex would complicate things.

I don't think sex would complicate things. It's not like we haven't done other stuff. Dad can be real weird about girls sometimes. Like he insists me and my brother, Rafael, act like "gentlemen" to women and girls, which means opening their door, letting them go first, helping them on with their coat. All this dumb stuff that Harper loves making us do. We have to practice on her.

Harper and Shayla hang on to the side of the pool, talking a mile a minute. I swim over to join them just as Harper says, "That's so cool!"

"What's so cool?" I ask.

Harper gets out of the pool, wringing her long brown hair out. "Shayla's stepping in for Kat Lopez in the lead role for *Angel Heart*." *Angel Heart* is a webcomic that was turned into a series of graphic novels. It's huge. A dark fantasy involving angels and demons.

Shayla gives me an uncertain smile. "It's a movie with a theatrical release. Pretty big."

I haul myself out of the pool and sit on the edge, patting the space next to me. She gives me her hand to help her out of the water and then yanks me in. I make a big splash to soak her.

She laughs and wraps her arms around my neck. "Now let's get to the kissing part."

Lust thunders through me. I pull her to where I can stand with my head above water and kiss her. She wraps her legs around me, and it feels so good I never want to stop kissing her.

She breaks the kiss a long while later. "Are you happy for me?"

"Course I am. *Angel Heart* is awesome. What happened to Kat Lopez?"

"She's got some kind of kidney condition that flared up. The thing is, I have to leave tomorrow to fly back to LA."

Not even her sexy body pressed so close can stop the chill that goes through me. "How long will you be gone?"

"Three months."

"Okay, but then you can come back. You could have Thanksgiving with us and Christmas and New Year. Maybe you could go to my school."

She strokes my cheek. "We'll see, okay? This could be a launch for me into more adult roles. Sometimes you have to build on that momentum. That's what my agent says, anyway."

"Is Mom okay with it?" I hate that I sound desperate, but Mom was the one who took Shayla in to keep her out of trouble in Hollywood. She's only been with us for two and a half months. Maybe Mom will say Shayla's not ready to go.

Shayla pulls away from me and gets out of the pool. I join her and grab two towels from the nearby patio table, handing her one. We dry off. I'm quiet, my throat tight, my chest aching. She's ripping my heart out. Does she even care about leaving me?

She wraps the towel around her body. "Your mom is happy for me. She wants to take me shopping this afternoon before I go. Harper's coming too."

I wrap the towel around my neck. "I hate shopping."

"I know. Let's meet up in the loft tonight, okay?" She grabs my head and kisses me passionately. I can't help myself, returning the kiss hungrily. Every time I'm with her, I just want to get closer and closer.

She shifts to whisper in my ear, "Bring a condom with you."

I still. "Are you sure?" She told me she had a bad first experience with a costar last year when she was fifteen. He was twenty-three. I want to kill that guy.

She kisses me again and gives me a sexy smile. "Yes. Absolutely."

I can barely breathe. That she would trust me like this. Yes! We're going to have sex. And it's not going to complicate things because this is right. Fortunately, I know what I'm doing on account of reading Mom's romance novels and trying stuff out on an enthusiastic fellow camp counselor last summer.

"See you tonight," she says.

I nod. And then I turn and watch her go, striding quickly into the house. This is going to be epic.

~

I prop up on an elbow and look down at Shayla's flushed face. "You good?" We're under a blanket on a sofa in the loft above the garage after the best sex ever. I can just make out her sparkling blue eyes in the dim glow from the security light attached to the garage outside.

She beams. "I'm great! I love you."

My heart pounds wildly. "I love you too."

She grabs my head and kisses me all over my face. I laugh, happier than I've ever been in my life.

I shift to my side next to her, and she lies on her side, facing me. I wrap an arm and leg around her, love and affection bursting through me.

I stroke her soft blond hair back from her face. "As soon as you're eighteen, we should get married."

"Owen—"

"We love each other. That means we should be together. I want to be with you forever."

"But that's two years away."

"We'll keep in touch. You can fly back here and stay with us when you're not working, and I'll come out there too. I've flown by myself before to visit my grandparents in North Carolina."

She kisses me. "You're so sweet. You really want to marry me?"

"I do." I laugh. "See? I already sound like a groom."

"We'll stay in touch."

"Nothing has to change. This is just a temporary separation."

She rolls away from me and pulls my arm around her middle. "Hold me just like this. I want to spend the whole night with you."

I spoon her, loving the way we fit together. "We'll have to sneak out early in the morning."

She reaches to the floor and sets an alarm on her phone before snuggling back into my arms. She sighs. "I could get used to this."

I nuzzle her neck and breathe in her sweet scent. "I love you."

She turns back to look at me. "I'll always love you, Owen."

Euphoria rushes through me. There's no other word for it. I'm suddenly wired, thinking about the future. Our future. I know we're young, but I'm sure we can make it work.

But in the hard light of day with Shayla's bags packed, and Mom ready to drive her to the airport, Shayla barely looks at me when she says goodbye. I get a very bad feeling about this.

5

———

Present day…

After speaking to the hotel manager of the SoHo Luxe Hotel, I set up a surveillance and alarm system that will tie to Shayla's and her bodyguard's phones, as well as the hotel's security. For now I'm her guard. Shayla's at work, filming just a few blocks away with Frankie as her guard while I work here. I got in touch with him to be sure all was well.

It's an interesting hotel, luxury with a vintage feel. The rooms are done in 1970s style, and the common areas down-stairs are 1950s style. They've made a big effort to make it interesting for creatives. Shayla's not the first celebrity to stay here. I would've preferred a less well-known celebrity hang-out. Someplace discreet, like an up-and-coming boutique hotel celebrities haven't discovered yet.

The penthouse suite is decorated to look like a 1970s artist loft with weathered oak floors and industrial touches like a concrete column in the large living room. I like the furniture. A long sectional sofa with too many pillows, multiple chairs, another smaller sofa. It's definitely a place meant to relax in with friends. There's a master bedroom and bath, a guest room with bath, a wet bar, and a terrace just off the living room with a great view of the Empire State Building.

A private-access elevator is already equipped with cameras and a key card activation. The entrance door is steel with a lever lock and key card combo. Later today, the strongest deadbolt lock available will be installed in the door. It's unbreakable and unpickable. This hotel is accommodating for celebrities' needs. It's how they stay in business.

By the end of the day, I've got the place wired and ready to go. I glance in the guest room, where I left my suitcase, and wander back to the living room, tempted by the wet bar. Not while I'm on the job. Now that I've finished the labor-intensive setup, the hard part starts, and I'm not talking about fighting whoever dares to hurt Shayla, I'm talking about living with the woman I've never been able to forget.

I head out of the suite, locking it securely behind me, and walk over to where they're filming today. It's a sunny May day in New York, and I relax immediately, being outside. If only it were safe to take Shayla out places, I could limit our roommate situation to just sleeping. I even checked out the viability of staying a floor below hers, but it was fully booked by some visiting dignitary.

A short while later, I give my name to the security guard on set. A production assistant wearing a headset shows up to escort me directly to where Shayla's filming in front of an Irish pub. She's in a black halter top exposing her muscled midriff. Wow, she really got ripped for this part. Her costar, Pete Hanson, a guy in his twenties wearing a T-shirt and jeans, is all smiles and charm. Reminds me a bit of my friend Nathan with his dark hair, blue eyes, and granite jaw.

I haven't seen Shayla acting since she was sixteen. When she moved in with us that summer, I had an instant massive crush and caught up on all her work. This was before she showed an interest in me. I'd been keeping my distance because Harper was with her all the time, and how could I make a move in front of my mouthy sister? Anyway, I've purposely avoided all of Shayla's films since then.

I watch as they film. She's improved a lot as an actor, and she was good before. There's a subtlety to her acting now, like she's learned to be more confident and fully inhabit the role. I know this stuff from Mom, who used to bring us to set when she was acting, and then later when she was producing and directing. She liked to talk shop with me and my siblings. I'm the only one who really listened. Not that it tempted me into the industry. Harper was always the dramatic one. She insisted on forging her own path as a graphic designer. She does a lot of corporate ads. Rafael's only twenty-two, but already a skilled photographer.

The director calls for another take, and the crew sets up the shot again. Pete moves in to talk to Shayla, making her laugh. I look away, annoyed for no good reason, and spot Frankie nearby.

I head over. "How's it going? Any Matt sightings?" I ran a full background check on her stalker. This is his first stalker situation. Apparently, he just discovered Shayla's work and became obsessed. I'd say he was lonely after his divorce, but most people look for someone new to date, not follow around an actor for a role she played eight years ago. He's thirty, no kids, and works freelance for a computer company. That means we need to pay attention to hacks. As appearances go, he looks like a mild-mannered guy—clean-shaven, short brown hair parted to the side, rectangular black-framed glasses.

"This morning there were a dozen roses waiting for her at the front desk," Frankie says grimly. "The card said: Katie, I can help you. Call me. He left his number this time, a Seattle area code." Katie is the name of the runaway character Shayla played when she was seventeen, the one Matt's obsessed with.

"We should move her."

"He's just going to track her down again."

I look around for anyone suspicious. "Have you seen him here?"

"No. He's good about staying out of sight. It's possible he changed his appearance. He used to reliably wear a black hoodie. He's gotten smarter, dressing like someone who goes to the office."

"Quiet on set," the director calls and gestures to the lighting guy.

Crew sounds off they're ready one by one. Background actors in place and—

"Action!" the director says.

I watch Shayla nail the scene again. It occurs to me that if she hadn't gotten her big break in *Angel Heart* when she was sixteen, she might not even have a career anymore. She'd just be one of the many former child stars unable to get work.

It was for the best. For both of us. I may have grown up around the industry, but that doesn't mean I want my life to revolve around it like it did for Dad. He sold his company and traveled around the world for Mom's work. Sure, he did other important work, helping to raise us kids, managing Mom's career, and running the business side of her production company. But that's not me. I need my own thing.

The scene ends, and the director calls it for the day. Frankie moves to Shayla's side, and they walk over to me together.

Shayla's intercepted by a PA, who fangirls over her. "Great work today, Shayla! It's so amazing the way you just become Tara. I'm taking an acting class, so I know how hard it is to be that authentic."

"Thank you, Paige," Shayla says. "And have fun with your class." Shayla never took classes. She learned on set as a child using her own instincts and outgoing personality. Mom did mention she had a private on-set coach for her first major movie role. The one she left us for. Welp, I'd been warned.

She walks over to me. The PA, Paige, stares at her with a look of awe. It's cool to have fans, as long as they don't cross the line.

"How long have you been here?" she asks me.

"Just enough to catch the last two takes."

"And?" she asks with a winning smile.

I steel my heart against that smile. "Fishing for compliments?"

"No, I was just curious what you thought."

"You've improved since you were sixteen."

Frankie snorts.

Shayla looks over her shoulder at him, probably shooting him a dark look since he's smiling widely now, before turning back to me. "You haven't seen my work since I was sixteen?"

"No, why would I?"

She opens her mouth and then shuts it. "Right. So I guess we should go. I'd like to walk since the hotel's close by." She turns to Frankie. "Thanks for your help today, Frankie. Tell Claire I said hi."

He inclines his head. "Will do." He clasps my arm in farewell and leaves.

"I just need to get my stuff from my trailer," she says.

I walk with her to her trailer. "Your suite is secured. I'll show you how to check the status on your phone and how to check in with your guard."

She enters a combination to get in the trailer, opens the door, and turns to me. "You're my guard."

"For now."

"No one asked you for forever."

She goes inside the trailer, and I follow her. She turns to face me, and we're suddenly real close. My pulse accelerates. I search her expression. It's hard to tell if she's happy I'm here. Maybe she didn't want me as much as I thought. Maybe she's plain scared and wanted an old friend near her.

"Hi," she says warmly.

"Nothing's going to happen between us," I say just to be clear.

She lifts her chin. "That would be unprofessional."

"Exactly."

"Owen?"

"Yeah?"

"I'm glad you'll be in my suite with me. Now I might

finally sleep through the night instead of waking in terror at every little sound."

"Aww, Shay."

She gives me a small smile. "Just need to do a quick change." She heads to the back of the trailer to a bedroom.

It's a big trailer similar to the kind Mom used to get. It means she has a lead role. There's a living room area with a table and chairs, a sofa bed, a small kitchen, a vanity setup for hair and makeup, as well as the bedroom and bathroom in back.

I wait, stuffing my hands in my jeans pockets while I try not to think about Shayla stripping just on the other side of that door.

A few moments later, she reappears in a T-shirt and jeans with her wardrobe on a hanger. She sets the hanger on a rod in a small closet.

"Wardrobe will stop by in the morning to clean and press it. They have two copies of this outfit."

"Uh-huh."

She slips her feet into heeled sandals and grabs her purse from the closet. "Ready."

"How's security on set?"

She leads the way out the door. "Good, I think. They've got several guards here to keep the public out. My trailer has a fancy lock."

I glance back at it. "What about the windows?"

"They have locks."

"I'm going to take a closer look at them tomorrow."

"Okay."

Several people stop to say hi to her as we leave the set location. One guy reminds her makeup time is eight a.m. tomorrow. Guess that means I'll be up early too. This is bringing back lots of childhood memories of being on set. It's a whole different world, but one that's familiar. I suppose that's good because I'm less likely to be starstruck by the setup and will notice when something's off.

On the walk back to the hotel, I ask her to tell me every

detail about the flowers and card that she can remember. After she does, she says, "And how was your day?"

"Busy. For your safety, you should avoid room service. Someone trusted will need to go out and get food. Do you have an assistant?"

"Yes, but she's in LA house-sitting for me."

"She needs to be here. She can take my room in the suite. I'll take the sofa."

"Yes, sir," she says crisply.

I keep a straight face. "Glad you're getting with the program."

~

Shayla

When we get to my hotel room, Owen finally stops lecturing me about stalker safety. Of course I know to be smart and not take any chances. Claire went over in great detail all she did to stay safe from her stalkers over the years.

An awkward silence stretches between us. Alone in a hotel suite. The bedroom mere steps away. I consider Owen my first, even though I wasn't a virgin at the time. My actual first experience at fifteen with my twenty-three-year-old costar was painful, quick, and ended with him bolting out the door. It was consensual, if not technically legal. I thought I was in love when really I was just desperately lonely and craving affection. Anyway, the next day on set he flirted with his makeup artist and pretended nothing had happened between us. Owen was my true first—slow and tender because he loved me. No one has ever topped that experience. True love makes all the difference.

He clears his throat, shifting uneasily.

"Can I get you anything to drink?" I gesture toward the wet bar. "It's fully stocked, and there's water and almond milk in the fridge."

"No, thanks." He looks around at everything but me. "So, I guess we're in for the night."

"We could go out if you want."

"No unnecessary trips until we have a handle on what Matt's capable of. I'm going to review the security footage from when he came in this morning and tell the staff not to let him in again."

"Frankie already took care of that."

"He left you alone on set to deal with stuff here?"

"Only for an hour while I was filming. There was security in place."

He shakes his head. "I want a guard with you at all times. I want to catch this asshole violating his restraining order. I'll let the local police know about it so we can act fast. Jail time might make him reconsider his obsession with you."

"Or at least give me a break for a few years."

He plants his hands on his hips. "Hopefully he'd get some counseling in prison that would redirect his focus."

Our gazes lock for a moment before he looks away. Another awkward silence.

"I can cook us dinner," I offer. "Stir-fry and brown rice. Would you like that?"

He looks toward the door like he wants to escape.

"You know you're not a prisoner here," I say. "Door's right there."

"I'm not leaving you until I know you have a reliable guard in place."

"Okay, well, I'm going to cook dinner."

"I'll check on some work email." He sounds so distant. I miss the warm, fun Owen. I know he must be in there somewhere.

He turns to go. I stare at the tense set of his shoulders. He's not comfortable with me after all the years that've passed between us. Would it help if I told him the truth? I never forgot him, never really got over him.

I ghosted him because it was too painful to have my heart with him, knowing I had to pursue my career no matter where in the world it took me. And I didn't think it would be fair to either of us to have a long-distance relationship. We were so young. I always hoped we'd reunite down the line when the timing was better and get back together. Maybe I should've said that back then.

But how could I make a promise I wasn't sure I could keep?

Now that we're older…God, I had this whole rosy future in mind. He'd forgive me, we'd pick up where we left off, and then we'd meld our careers together. I'd get him security work for the movie studios I work for, and he'd travel with me from set to set around the world. Mackenzie told me their company was looking to expand to new industries. My career would boost his. I confess that Claire's happy marriage to Jake made me dream big. Fantasies. Ridiculous fantasies.

Still, I have to do something to bridge this distance. We were close once.

"Owen?"

He turns, his expression reserved.

I step closer. "I know we didn't leave things on the best of terms between us. I'm sorry—"

"Don't be. I'm over it."

He turns on his heel and heads into the guest room, shutting the door behind him. I stare at the closed door, my mind scrambling for how to fix this.

If he won't accept my apology, how else can I make things up to him?

6
———

The next three nights are, unfortunately, more of the same with Owen. Every time I try to make the conversation more personal, he shuts it down. I've been cooking dinner for him every night as part of my *look, I've changed* plan. (I didn't know how to cook when I was younger.) I heard the way to a man's heart is through his stomach, but that is not the case with Owen. He wolves down his food and retreats to his room, shutting the door behind him.

As much time as we spend together, basically twenty-four seven, the distance between us feels greater than ever. I might as well be back in LA for all he notices me. The only time he speaks is in answer to a direct question or to fill me in on my security status. At least his constant presence has kept Matt away. Probably the steely-eyed stare Owen gives to our surroundings at all times.

We're settled in for another silent night back at the hotel suite, so I text him from the living room. *You're the best body-guard I could ask for.*

Multiple texts come back.

Owen: *Don't get used to it.*

Has your assistant found anyone good?

Where the hell is she, anyway?

Owen's mad it's taking so long for Olivia to get here. Probably because he doesn't want to be alone with me.

I sigh and walk over to his bedroom door, talking through it. "I told you she'll be here on Sunday. She has her niece's birthday party on Saturday. I do let my employees have a personal life."

"Not me."

"That was your choice." I clench my jaw. "Take the day off tomorrow. Your sister and cousin will be here. That's plenty to scare off Matt."

The door swings open, and we're suddenly up close and personal. I suck in air, every part of my body heating at the sight of Owen in a snug T-shirt and shorts. His skin's sort of glowing. I wonder if he was working out in there.

"You didn't tell me they'd be here," he says. "You're supposed to keep me updated on your schedule. We have a shared calendar."

"Sorry, I'm not used to updating a calendar. Olivia keeps on top of stuff like that for me."

He stares at me for a moment before saying, "Guess you're still close with them."

"Yeah. I love your family and all the get-togethers we had in Clover Park. It was the happiest summer of my life."

His jaw clenches. "I'll be in the lounge downstairs while they're here." He takes a step back and shuts the door in my face.

"We'll miss you!" I yell through the door. *Not.*

Silence.

I barely resist kicking the door. Forget a second chance with him. I don't know what I was thinking. The man is a stone wall, no humor, no warmth. This is not the Owen Campbell I remember.

I head back to the sofa and turn on the TV to the cooking channel. A text pings on my phone.

Owen: *Mackenzie and Harper won't miss me. I see them all the time. Guess it's you.*

My pulse flutters. He's reaching out! Finally!

Me: *I missed you a lot over the years. I never forgot you.*

I hold my breath. Three dots appear while he's typing.

They disappear.

I've said too much. Dammit. I've always been an emotional person prone to sharing too soon. That's why acting is such a great outlet for me. This must be the problem with all of my relationships. I say how I feel, and the other person doesn't feel the same way, so they back off. Or they feel more strongly than I do, and I have to let them down gently.

Let's face it, no one's ever lived up to my memory of Owen.

Maybe Mackenzie and Harper can help me understand the man he is today.

"Welcome to Chez Adler!" I say, letting Harper and Mackenzie into my suite. It's Saturday afternoon. Owen met them at the private elevator and then rode it down to the lobby.

"Fancy!" Harper says, looking over my shoulder at the suite. "Just like you, Miss Fancy Pants." She kisses my cheek and steps into the living room.

Mackenzie hugs me. "It's been too long, woman."

I beam at them. The pair are cousins, but could pass as sisters, something about their facial features. Probably because their dads—Jake and Josh—are identical twins. Their coloring is different, though. Harper has long honey-brown hair and hazel eyes while Mackenzie has brown hair and blue eyes. "I missed you ladies. Who wants champagne?"

"You have to ask?" Harper says, flopping in the center of the sofa. "Wow, I feel like this sofa could swallow me whole. It's so squishy. Awesome hotel, by the way. The bar and lounge look so retro."

Mackenzie takes a seat next to Harper and crosses her legs. "I prefer B&Bs. You get to stay in a house."

Harper wrinkles her nose. "Yeah, but then you have to eat breakfast with random strangers."

"Who could one day lead to potential clients," Mackenzie returns.

Harper gives Mackenzie's hair a tug. "Always be networking, huh, cuz?" She turns toward the terrace and whistles. "Fantastic view, too. Can we go out there?"

I head to the kitchen for the champagne. "Owen doesn't want me on the terrace with my stalker situation."

"But if your stalker shoots you, what would he do with all his time?" Harper quips.

"Harper!" Mackenzie exclaims.

She lifts her palms. "Sorry, Shay, that was in poor taste. Sometimes things sound funnier in my head than out loud."

"I'll let you know when you finally achieve funny." I don't take offense. Harper's grown up with her mom's stalkers and paparazzi, so she takes it in stride.

"Like never," Mackenzie says.

I open the champagne. *Pop!*

"Woot! Party time!" Harper exclaims.

I pour us each a glass and sit on the end of the sofa next to Harper. Mackenzie's on her other side. "A toast to old friends. I missed you."

"Who're you calling old?" Harper asks.

"I'm the youngest," Mackenzie says, preening. "When you ladies turn thirty, I'll still be in my twenties."

"Please, you'll be twenty-nine," I say. "Can we toast now?"

"To good friends," Harper says, lifting her glass.

We clink glasses and drink to that.

"So tell us what's new in Hollywood," Mackenzie says. "What's Collin Quincy like in real life?"

"God, Mac, you're obsessed with him," Harper says. "You realize he's not actually a Scottish warrior, right?"

Mackenzie sighs. "Mac is a truck or a trucker. It's Mackenzie." She turns to me expectantly. "So?"

I smile. "He's very nice and professional. His wife and twin daughters frequently visited the set."

Mackenzie smiles dreamily. "That just makes him more irresistible. A family man. Not that I'm looking for that any time soon. Now is the time for fun."

Harper nudges Mackenzie. "You're killing your mom with that attitude."

"She'll live." Mackenzie turns to me. "Anyway, how are you?"

I fill them in on my latest work on *Breakdown,* and the movie I've booked in Vancouver right after this, an indie film called *The Highlighter* about an art dealer. "You should visit me there. Vancouver is gorgeous."

"I grew up around sets," Harper says. "Nothing more boring than watching everyone set up and do the same scene over and over."

"I think it would be fun," Mackenzie says.

I give her arm a squeeze. "Great!"

"You'd probably be working the whole time anyway." Harper's voice holds a note of FOMO.

I take her hand and kiss the back of it. "I'd make special time for you."

She flutters her lashes. "With an invitation like that, how can I say no?"

We clink glasses again.

I bring in veggies and dip for nourishment while we catch up on each other's lives. Harper tells us about her work as a graphic designer while Mackenzie fills us in on the latest with Brooks Campbell Security.

"Speaking of which, how's the living situation with Owen?" Harper asks casually. They both know we were together as teens, though I never shared the details. It felt private and special. Just between me and Owen.

I slice a hand through the air. "Strictly professional."

"Bummer."

"Of course he's professional," Mackenzie says. "She hired him for a security gig. Securing this place and guard duty."

She turns to me. "You've got him until next Friday provided you have a suitable replacement for him."

I'm fully aware time is running out. It's already less than a week left. "My assistant's looking into it. I'm sure she'll find somebody soon."

Harper sips her champagne. "Shay, you could've just asked Mom for a bodyguard referral. She knows everyone."

I take a deep breath. "Honestly, I'm hoping for a second chance with Owen."

They both stare at me, eyes wide. I'm taken aback for a moment. I thought they knew Owen was the love of my life. Didn't the fact that I haven't had a serious relationship since Owen show that no one could compare? Don't they remember how happy we were together back then?

"Why do you look so shocked?" I ask.

"You broke his heart," Harper says.

"He doesn't believe in love anymore," Mackenzie says. "Because of you."

My stomach drops like a stone. I cross my arms tightly, hugging myself. He doesn't believe in love? I did that?

"I feel terrible," I say. "I never stopped believing in love. I thought..." I trail off at their sympathetic looks, my throat tight. All I can remember is how madly in love we were back then.

I swallow hard. "I didn't mean to destroy his faith in love. He loved me, and I loved him, but what were we supposed to do about it back then? I was sixteen; he was seventeen."

"That is young," Harper says. "I shudder to think about still being with my boyfriend from when I was sixteen."

"Right?" Mackenzie says. "You've always had the worst taste in men."

"Hey!" Harper tosses a baby carrot at Mackenzie's head. She catches it and chomps on it.

Harper huffs. "At least I didn't wait until I was twenty-three to get a boyfriend like some people."

Mackenzie lifts her chin. "So I had standards." She sighs. "And then Shawn disappointed them, and I said to myself,

self, why not just have fun and not worry so much about meeting the perfect guy, and that's what I've been doing ever since. No expectations means no heartache."

Harper inclines her head. "That's fair. After Brian, I see the wisdom in that move." Brian was Harper's client, who became her live-in boyfriend of two years until she came home to find him in bed with another woman. Her friend and coworker. What an idiot. Brian, not Harper.

"So what brought this on?" Harper asks me. "Why do you want a second chance with my bro? She asks innocently with a hint of—" she drops her voice to a low threatening tone "— hurt him again and I'll kill you." She narrows her eyes at me.

"Because I always hoped when the timing was right, we'd get back together. He loved me once." I swallow over the lump of emotion lodged in my throat. "He's the only one I know for sure truly did. I suppose his love for me…died. I chose to take that movie gig, and now I have to live with the fact that I may have lost him forever." My eyes get hot.

Harper and Mackenzie give me sympathetic looks.

I finish my champagne in one long drink. "I was still very much a work-in-progress back then. The pressures of the industry, recovering from Mom's emotional abuse, just recently sober and drug-free, I'm not even sure I could've sustained a relationship. It was all I could do to stay strong and make a life for myself." I take a deep breath. "I'm in a better place now. I would do things differently this time, if he'd give me a chance."

"I'm sure it would be nice for you to be with someone familiar who's not in the industry," Mackenzie says.

I shake my head. "It's not about him being familiar. He's special."

"He's alright," Harper says, pouring me more champagne. High praise from his sister.

I take them both in. "I see him all the time, and he's more distant by the minute. I'm at a loss. I get it, he doesn't want a relationship, but couldn't we at least be friends?" My voice cracks.

Harper and Mackenzie exchange a look.

Harper shakes her head. "You can't be friends once you've had sex. Everybody knows that. Oh, did you think I didn't know about the late-night loft meetups?"

I wince. "Did your mom know?"

"Nah, the parents were sound asleep. I was the night owl hearing you sneak out. I followed you once and saw you meet up with him in front of the garage, and then up you go to the loft. My parents cluelessly made it a playroom slash gamer den for us kids. They really should've known we'd use it for all sorts of unsupervised fun."

I look out to the view. "Part of me wishes I could go back in time and do things differently. Maybe if I'd stayed in touch, or I don't know…something."

After a moment, Mackenzie says, "You should come to the anniversary slash double college graduation party at Happy Endings tonight with us. It'll give us a chance to watch you with Owen, and we could let you know if you have a chance in hell with him. You're probably too close to the situation to see things clearly."

"You should come just to have fun with us," Harper says. "Frankie will be there with Mom, so Owen can have a break from all his vigilance."

"He'll definitely be more relaxed at a family event," Mackenzie says.

Hope sneaks in and wraps around my heart once more. "That sounds like a plan. Rafael graduated, right? Who else?"

"Michael," Harper says. "Do you remember my aunt Mad's sons? The four *M*s?"

I smile. "Oh, yeah, Michael, the identical twins, and there was another one. Remind me of their names."

"Mason, Michael, Maddox, and Miles," Mackenzie says. "Maddox and Miles are the twins. I'd like to point out I was the first *M*."

"Aunt Mad was the first *M*," Harper says. "And the first Mackenzie was actually born two days before you."

"Damn, you're right. I'm not even the first Mackenzie in

the family. I blame a lack of communication between brothers."

"Huh?" I ask.

"My uncle Ty's baby was born two days before me," Mackenzie says. "They had to go to Louisiana to adopt her from the birth mom, and named her there. No one here knew the name until they returned a few days later, and by that time I was born and named Mackenzie too. My cousin goes by Kenzie."

"That's cute," I say.

Mackenzie dips a piece of celery. "We have way too many *M* names in our family."

"It was Aunt Mad's way of naming four sons after herself," Harper says. "I guess if she had a daughter, she would've named her Madison. Then she'd probably have to give her a cutesy nickname like Maddie so it wouldn't be confused with Mad, and then poor Maddie would be stuck with a kiddy name instead of a badass name like Mad."

"It's like a dad named Dick naming his son Dick," Mackenzie says. "Then you forever have Big Dick and Little Dick."

We crack up.

"Poor Little Dick," Harper gasps out.

Mackenzie holds up a palm. "I swear, true story. Mom had a client's dad named Big Dick just recently. And his son was Little Dick, who was trying to get everyone to call him Richard instead."

"Oh my God!" I exclaim.

I laugh until my stomach hurts. Finally, I calm down and wipe my eyes. "Wow, I needed that. So whose anniversary is it? I want to make sure my gifts are personalized."

"No gifts," Harper says. "There's too many of us to always be buying everyone gifts. We all chip in on a single gift. Anyway, you'll be our guest, so no need to chip in."

I swallow hard. "Oh."

"What?" Harper asks.

I shrug. "When I used to live here, I kinda felt like part of the family." My voice sounds small. Maybe I was always the outsider. Maybe my memories of the Campbell family and Clover Park are just nostalgic longing.

"Of course you're part of the family!" Harper exclaims.

Mackenzie nods. "Everyone chips in twenty."

I brighten. "I can do that. Who's the anniversary couple?"

"Grandpop Joe and Grandmom Brandy," Mackenzie says. "Mom never thought they'd last, but they've been happily married for seventeen years."

I remember this family story because it was so unusual. Josh's dad, Joe, met and fell in love with Hailey's mom, Brandy, later in life. They got engaged, forcing Josh and Hailey to make amends after a long, contentious frenemies deal. And then, finally, Josh and Hailey fell in love too. They're technically stepsiblings, but no one dares bring it up. Speaking of a frenemies deal…

"So what's the latest with Nathan?" I ask Harper.

She sniffs. "I guess we'll find out tonight. I haven't seen him since last year when he told me my sundress looked like something an old woman would wear."

"Because he wanted you in something skintight," Mackenzie says with a sigh. "You have to read between the lines."

"Nathan Brooks is a jerk," Harper says. "Why're we even talking about him?"

Mackenzie shakes her head. "You didn't think he was a jerk when you met him in second grade. You told me he was your best friend."

Harper bristles. "Second-grade me was an idiot. Fortunately, I have much better taste in friends now." She reaches one arm around Mackenzie and one arm around me. "Like you ladies."

Mackenzie laughs. "Unless there's a spider in the vicinity, and then it's every woman for themselves." She turns to me. "She knocked me off the sofa trying to get away from a spider once."

"How about when you crashed into me on roller skates

while I was on my pogo stick?" Harper returns. "You know you wanted that pogo stick. Couldn't wait your turn, as usual."

And they're off.

"You're the one who never took turns, hogging Nikki's Corvette," Mackenzie says. "Always trying to make me be the boring guy doll with no car."

"It was *my* Corvette!"

I smile as they throw out past incidents from childhood, where the other wronged them in the way only sisters could. God, I love these ladies. If anyone can help me figure out this thing with Owen, it's them.

7

Owen

I finish getting ready in Shayla's guest room and step out to the living room. Shayla's bedroom door is open, but I won't cross that line.

I call loudly enough for her to hear, "Will Frankie be here soon? I don't want to be late for the party." I roll up the cuffs of my white dress shirt. "I'll be back to relieve him by midnight."

She steps out of the bedroom in a sleeveless black dress, modest on top, but ending high on her thigh. My mouth goes dry as my gaze drifts down her bare toned legs to black-heeled sandals with straps that wrap around her ankles. I stare at those sexy legs in a sensual haze, imagining touching, kissing, and tasting all that skin.

"Actually, I'm going to the party too."

My gaze jerks up to hers. *No way.* This was the one night I could relax without worrying about her safety. And let's face it, without being tempted. I need space away from her to strengthen my willpower. I'm not sure if she's doing it on purpose, but she seems to be wearing skimpier pajamas every night. Last night she wore what looked like a short silk dress that barely covered her ass.

She finishes putting a silver dangling earring in. "Mackenzie and Harper invited me. I told Frankie we'd meet him there."

"No." It comes out harsher than I mean it to. "You can't go to the party."

"I didn't ask you for permission. I'm going. You should be happy that Frankie will be at the party with your mom now."

"You're not family. This is a family party."

A flash of hurt crosses her face, but then she lifts her chin. "Claire is like a second mom to me. She's happy I'm going to be there. She said the only reason she didn't invite me is because she thought I'd be overwhelmed by the chaos. She still remembers me at sixteen when I needed alcohol to get through a party. I'm good now."

I clench my jaw. "So now I can't relax because I'll be working."

"Frankie will be working. You'll be living it up. I've got a car waiting downstairs for us. Are you ready?"

"Yeah, I'm ready," I grumble.

"Great! Let me just get my purse."

She returns a moment later with a tiny beaded purse on a chain.

"What could you possibly carry in that purse?" I ask her as I open the door and check the hallway.

"That's a very personal question."

My lips curve up, but I hide it by striding ahead to the private elevator. "How is that personal?" I do the elevator code, and the doors open.

She steps into the elevator. "Because a purse is meant to stash things you don't want everyone to see. Otherwise, I'd be carrying my stuff in a clear plastic bag."

I follow her in and press the button. She looks straight ahead, ignoring me.

I tell myself to enjoy the quiet, but I can't help teasing her. "I bet you have a phone and a hundred-dollar bill in there."

"A hundred-dollar bill isn't very useful for tipping."

"And lipstick."

She turns to face me and opens her purse. There's two things—her phone and pepper spray. She's protecting herself. I have the urge to pull her into my arms and tell her everything will be okay, and at the same time, I'm proud of her for carrying it.

She shuts the purse. "And there's a small inner pocket with a condom. Now you know."

My jaw goes slack. I wish I didn't know because now all I can think about is wanting to be the one to use it with her. I'd say she purposely put the sexy image in my mind, but I'm the dope who had to know what was in her purse.

The doors open, and she strides out, her heels clicking on the tile floors of the hallway leading out to the lobby.

I scope out the hallway and open the door to the lobby, taking a look around before stepping out and holding the door for her.

The front desk clerk gives her a warm smile. "Good evening, Miss Adler."

"Have a good night, Bertie," she says.

He beams. "Thank you."

She remembers everyone's name and makes sure to use it. People seem to love it. I guess that's how she got my attention in the beginning. Overusing my name, which made me think she was into me.

The car out front is the same Mercedes with tinted windows as before. We haven't used it this week since we've been walking to her work a short distance away. The driver gets out when he sees us. "Everything's as requested."

He opens the back door for Shayla.

"Thank you, Martin," she says with a sunny smile. The woman knows how to use her charm, but that won't work on me.

I follow her into the backseat, where there's a large bowl of my favorite snack—popcorn with peanut M&M's. *She remembered.* There's also champagne chilling in a bucket in the center console. My stomach growls. I planned to eat at the party, where there's always plenty of food, but this is looking pretty good.

"Is this for me?" I ask.

The car pulls away from the curb.

She gives me a small smile. "You got me hooked on the popcorn-peanut M&M's combo. It's for both of us. Tonight's a cheat night for me. Help yourself." She opens the champagne and pours a plastic glass, offering it to me.

I take it. "Does champagne really go with popcorn?"

"The fizziness is the perfect contrast to the salty and sweet. Try it." She pours herself a glass.

I take some popcorn and M&M's, chew, and wash it down with the champagne. "Pretty good."

"Pretty good? It's excellent."

I eat some more, reminded of movie nights in the basement of my house growing up. "Remember when we watched *Blue Force* and Harper cried at the end?"

She holds up a finger. "And she denied it, even though we could see her eyes were shiny with tears."

"So stupid. Crying at an alien horror movie just because Lauren left in their ship."

Shayla laughs. "She said it was because she thought she'd die alone out there."

"It was supposed to be a happy ending. She wanted to experience their culture."

She fist-bumps me. "Remember *Once and Always*?" That was a romantic movie she wanted to watch. Harper didn't want to see it, and my parents were at a school event for Rafael, so that left me. That night was the hottest, sexiest time imaginable between us—first in a chair and then on the bar top. Insane chemistry coupled with insane lust. I've never wanted someone so bad in my life.

I meet her eyes. "We didn't see much of that one."

"No," she says softly. So soft I find myself leaning in. She smells citrusy and something uniquely her. My gaze drops to her luscious lips, my heart thudding in my ears.

I lift a hand to her cheek. Her skin is so soft. I forgot how soft. She leans into my palm, closing her eyes. She wants me to kiss her. *I* want to kiss her. So what's stopping me?

I drop my hand. I let myself get in too deep once, and I swore I'd never let it happen again. I'm smarter than that. Anyway, I don't kid myself she'll be sticking around long.

She looks down at my hand, gives it a squeeze, and goes back to eating popcorn. I let out a breath. The moment's passed.

"I still don't know how that movie ends," she says.

"I'm sure they got together."

"Thanks for the spoiler!"

I laugh, relieved we're back to joking around. I toss back champagne. "This is growing on me. Beats the flavored sparkling water we always had in the fridge for movie nights." Mom never let us have soda, saying it was the worst thing for our teeth and bodies. When I finally had soda at a friend's house, I didn't like it. Guess it's an acquired taste.

"You guys had the healthiest food and drinks at home all the time."

"Except for movie night. I think that's how Mom got us kids to always want to have it. Like a family tradition."

She sighs. "My family tradition was a daily torture routine of beauty treatments. Mom highlighted my hair, did facials, brow waxing, skin toners, fat reducers, manicures, and pedicures. I was an immaculately made-up child."

I suppress a wince. She didn't have it easy growing up an only child with her mom. "Are you still in touch with her?"

"She died."

I put a hand on her arm in sympathy. Her warm bare arm. I quickly drop it. "I'm sorry. I didn't know."

"Yeah, about five years ago. Cancer. Honestly, I didn't feel much about it. We hadn't been in touch for years. I was still working through the emotional abuse and control she exerted over me. For a while, I felt guilty for not feeling sad enough. Now I've just accepted I feel what I feel, and that's okay."

"Sounds like someone's been to therapy."

She elbows me. "Don't knock it 'til you've tried it."

"Nah, it's good. I know it was hard for you growing up despite all the glamour of being a child star."

"I don't regret working as a kid. I think I would've gone insane without that outlet, and now I'm happy to have the career I have."

We're quiet as we eat, our hands occasionally brushing as we reach for popcorn at the same time. I don't hate it. Okay, okay, I like it. Every touch just makes me want more. What if I acted on impulse? Kissed her, pulled her under me, slid my hand—

"I'm sorry about the way things ended between us."

Now that's a splash of cold water. Lust killed. *Thanks, I needed that.*

I concentrate on refilling my champagne, watching the bubbles rise. "Don't worry about it. We were kids."

"I didn't know how to handle all I was feeling, and I didn't know about the future for me, for you, for my career. I just couldn't make any promises I wasn't sure I could keep."

I want to say that my marriage proposal didn't count, but that would be a lie. I loved her deeply and wanted to marry her. If we'd stayed in touch, visiting regularly, I think we would've been good together. Now it's different. We're different.

I keep it light. "It's okay. I forgive you for giving up the best you've ever had."

"You *are* the best I've ever had," she says so sincerely I'm shocked into silence. Me at seventeen was the best she ever had? She's been with the elite, with all the looks and all the money.

I go back to eating popcorn and M&M's. No more hand touching.

"I did it again," she says, rubbing her forehead. "I always share too much too soon."

It occurs to me she's acting, trying to reel me in with compliments and fake angst about oversharing. Well, I won't be fooled.

"Save it," I say.

"Save what?"

"You're acting. I'm not falling for that shit."

Her jaw drops. "What are you talking about?"

"Come on. Best you ever had when I was seventeen compared to—forget it. Past is past. It is what it is. And now we're here. You're paying me to protect you, and that lasts exactly one more week."

She huffs. "You're an idiot."

"I'm the idiot who's going to make sure you're safe."

"Yeah, for one more week," she says sourly.

"I'll find you a bodyguard. Your assistant is being way too slow about that. She should've had a list by now."

"She does have a list."

"Why haven't I seen it?"

"Because you didn't need to see it."

"Course I did. I need to make sure they're qualified."

She goes back to picking M&M's out of the popcorn. "That's what she's doing. She's calling references and interviewing them."

I lean toward her, living dangerously. Her breath hitches. That telltale sign of desire shouldn't thrill me as much as it does. "And?"

Her eyes meet mine. "So far no one has met my criteria."

"And what's that?"

She waves a hand in the air. "They're not—"

"Not me? Shayla, let me be clear, you're never going to have me. This is a temporary gig I'm doing as a favor."

Her eyes flash. "I was going to say they're not experienced enough. Someone is full of himself."

"Oh. I—"

She puts up a palm. "Just go back to eating popcorn. I don't want to hear one more rude thing out of your mouth."

"You're rude."

"Oh, very mature. I say you're rude, and then you say it."

"You're rude for hogging all the peanut M&M's."

She looks down at the bowl, which is pretty sparse on

M&M's. "I'm sure there's more on the bottom." She always hogged the M&M's.

It's nice to know some things haven't changed. There's still some small part of the girl I once knew and loved. Too bad she cared more about her career, hell, even my family than me.

8

―――――――

Owen's being a jerk. I sincerely apologized and shared from the heart that he was the best I've ever had. Because he *loved* me. It showed in every touch and every kiss. But what's the point of sharing with a man who's so suspicious of my intentions, he thinks I'm acting when I pour my heart out? Tears sting my eyes. I'm not a fake. I would never…I swallow hard, pushing the emotions down. I can't fall apart now when I'm about to go to a party with his family.

I stare out the window as the car drives down Main Street in Clover Park. My memory is of a quaint New England town centered around Main Street with shops and restaurants, and it looks exactly the same. That's nice.

The name Happy Endings in deep red stands out on a sign over the restaurant. Through the large front windows, I can see lots of people already gathered. Balloons with Congratulations! bounce cheerfully in a light breeze from the front railing.

The car pulls around the block to park in back. Owen bolts out the door as soon as we park like he can't wait to get away from me.

I take a deep breath and follow him out.

"Let's go." He places a hand on my lower back and

hurries me through the parking lot to the back door of the restaurant.

"I wanted to go in the front like everyone else. Clover Park is safe. Your mom says she stops by regularly to meet with the Happy Endings Book Club."

He lets out a breath, grumbles something I can't quite hear, and then hustles me around the building to the front. He opens the door for me and lets me go in first. He always had gentleman manners, something his dad taught him and his brother. I like it.

The moment I step inside Happy Endings, I'm enveloped in warmth and cheeriness. I was here a couple of times before. To my right is the restaurant area with several booths and tables, where a bunch of Campbells are gathered talking and laughing. There's a long buffet set up too. Straight ahead is a long wraparound dark cherrywood bar, which is also packed.

"I see Frankie," Owen says, guiding me over to him in the dining area. "Hey, Frankie, thanks for understanding about the change in plans."

Frankie inclines his shaved head. "No problem."

"She's all yours." And with that, Owen dumps me, heading straight for the bar.

He's greeted by the bartender with a slap on the back. That must be Cooper, Mackenzie's younger brother, all grown up. He's handsome in a down-to-earth kind of way— rumpled honey brown hair, scruffy jaw.

I look around. "Let's go see Claire."

Frankie gestures toward where Claire's standing with a group of women around her age. We make our way through the crowd to her. Owen's aunts, uncles, and cousins were frequent visitors at Claire's house, so I recognize a couple of people right away. There's Owen's aunt Hailey, a wedding planner and former beauty queen. She looks nearly the same, fit with long strawberry blonde hair and just a few lines around her pale blue eyes.

Next to her is Owen's aunt Madison with a short bob of brown hair and sharp brown eyes. She scared me the first time I met her. Probably didn't help that she said, "Owen's got a heart of gold, so don't hurt him or I will take you out." I don't think she was kidding either. A bloodthirsty woman I'd never want to piss off.

Claire hugs me. "So glad you could make it. If you survive tonight, I'll get you on the list for all the premier Campbell events."

I smile. "I've really made it now."

"Right?" She takes in my dress with a whistle. "We're casual here, but if that doesn't catch his eye, I don't know what will." Claire figured out I had more than one reason for hiring Owen, and she's rooting for me. I hadn't told her up front because I didn't want to get her hopes up if it didn't work out. My own hopes are in the gutter.

"He couldn't wait to get away from me," I say. "He dropped me off with Frankie and headed straight for the bar."

She looks over at the bar and smiles. "Well, he's looking at you now, so that's a good sign."

Hailey perks up, her blue eyes shining with excitement. "Ooh, are we talking a good sign of love? I've been hoping Owen would find a nice woman, and it looks like he found you again. It's fate! Oh, and congratulations on all your success, Shayla. Did you know Claire regularly has screenings at her house of your movies so the Happy Endings Book Club can watch them together?"

My cheeks warm. I glance at Claire, who shrugs. I take in the group of women all smiling at me. "No, I didn't know that. Thank you."

Claire puts an arm around me. "What can I say? I'm proud of her. Not that I had much to do with it, but—"

"You had everything to do with it." My voice cracks with emotion. If it weren't for Claire, I would've continued a downward spiral and ended up in a really dark place. "You taught me everything I needed to know about surviving and thriving in the industry."

Claire puts a hand to her heart. "Is that all? Well, you

deserve every good thing that's come your way. I know you work hard."

"True."

We smile at each other. She always said we had to work hard to carve out a place for ourselves, that Hollywood was not always easy for women, and we had to be able to hold our heads high with the choices we make. I suppose that's good advice for women in any line of business. She's basically a genius mentor, friend, and adopted mom all wrapped in one.

"Hey, Shayla," Madison says. "Heard you were in town and hired Owen. So are you two back together?" She looks over at him and waves. Then she yells, "Yes, we're talking about you!"

Oh my God. I glance over, but Owen's turned away.

Madison grins. "Nothing keeps a man away better than knowing a bunch of women are talking about him. So, what's the deal?"

I smooth my hair back. "Nothing, really. He's working for me temporarily because of a stalker situation, and…" I hesitate to call us friends. I don't think he likes to be around me all that much. Though there was a brief moment in the car when I thought he might kiss me. "And that's it," I finish lamely.

Hailey grabs my arm. "I can help you."

My heart thumps harder. Hailey's reputation as a matchmaker precedes her, though I doubt Owen would be swayed by anything his aunt said. "That's not necessary. Things are good just the way they are."

"Shay!" Harper calls from across the room. "Get over here, woman!"

Oh, thank God. "I've got to go. So nice to see you ladies again, and thanks for watching my movies. I appreciate it."

Madison points at me. "See if you can do more movies where you're a kickass action hero like in *Angel Heart*. Maybe get into a superhero franchise."

"My next movie is an action hero. She's in the military."

"Cool!"

Someone tugs my hair from behind.

I turn, and Harper hugs me. "Come with me," she whispers in my ear. "Mackenzie's flirting with a waiter. It's hysterical."

I follow her to the buffet, where a young guy with short dark hair and a tribal tattoo wrapped around one swollen bicep is replacing hot food dishes.

Mackenzie's just across from him. "Ooh, that looks good. What is it?"

He points to the card in front of the tray. "Cavatelli with broccoli."

"Is there any meat in it? I'm thinking of becoming a vegetarian."

"Doesn't look like it."

She follows him to the next tray that he's busy removing. "Do you live in town? I do."

"Yup."

"Where at?"

He meets her eyes with a smile. "Why, you want to visit me?"

She looks up at him under her lashes. "Maybe."

He heads back to the kitchen with the empty tray.

Mackenzie turns to us. "Isn't he gorgeous? Did you see his tattoo? I'm thinking he'd be a lot of fun."

"Anyone can get a tattoo," Harper says drily. "It doesn't make him hot."

Mackenzie turns to me for my opinion.

"It would probably be good to know more about him first."

She waves that away. "Dad hired him, and he vets everyone carefully."

"Who did I hire?" her dad asks, appearing out of nowhere. I could pick out Owen's uncle Josh anywhere because he's an identical twin to Owen's dad, Jake. Same short dark brown hair with a wave to it, warm brown eyes, and a mischievous smile. Josh dresses casually, mostly in T-shirts and jeans, whereas his twin, Jake, favors designer outfits. They share a similar sense of humor and finish each other's sentences.

Mackenzie gives her dad a bright smile. "The waiter with the tribal tattoo on his bicep, brown hair. I didn't catch his name."

"Harry."

"He seems nice," she says. "I know you vet everyone thoroughly before hiring."

Jake appears next to Josh. "Who seems nice?"

Josh shrugs. "My new waiter."

"Nice as in 'can I date him, Dad?'" Jake asks Josh.

"Mackenzie's an adult," Josh says. "She doesn't need my permission to date, but she might want to check in with his boyfriend, my sous chef."

Josh and Jake exchange mischievous smiles. It's hard to know when they're being serious. Harper suppresses a laugh.

Mackenzie parks a hand on her hip. "I know you're just saying that because you think he's not good enough for me, like all men."

Josh puts his hands up. "Don't shoot the messenger." He offers his hand to me. "Hey, Shayla, good to see you again. I heard you were back in town."

I shake his hand. "Good to be here. I love this place."

He smiles widely. "I do too. You know I worked my way up from bartender to manager to owner. Cooper's doing the same now."

"No easy path for Cooper," Jake says.

"Like you would just hand your kids their future," Josh returns.

"You have to work hard for what you want," they say at the same time.

"More Grandpop Joe words of wisdom," Mackenzie tells me. "He's got lots of great sayings that Dad and Uncle Jake like to use on us."

Josh slings an arm around Mackenzie's shoulders and kisses the top of her head. "Because it's good advice. Did you wish him and Grandmom Brandy a happy anniversary?"

"First thing."

Josh inclines his head toward the back of the restaurant. "Rafael and Michael are in the back room, playing pool. Stop by to say congrats to them too."

Mackenzie smiles sweetly. "I will."

He leaves with Jake, heading for their wives.

Mackenzie turns to me and Harper. "Do you think he was messing with me, or is Harry gay?"

"Hard to tell," I say.

"Only one way to find out," Harper says.

Mackenzie groans and shifts to the buffet, filling a plate with food. "Dad's put me in an awkward position. I either have to ask the sous chef…Trey, that's his name, if he's in a relationship with Harry, or ask Harry if he's single and likes women. Ugh."

Harper and I grab plates too and work down the line with her. Ooh, asparagus and pepper salad.

"Or you could just throw yourself at Harry and see what happens," Harper says cheerfully.

Mackenzie sighs. "It's not easy to meet guys when you live in a small town and most of your social life revolves around family events."

"There's always online dating," I say. "I've heard it works for some people."

"I'm not looking for anything serious," Mackenzie says.

"There's an app for that too," Harper returns, whipping out her phone to show Mackenzie.

Mackenzie crinkles her nose. "I like to meet guys in real life so I can see if there's a good vibe there."

"I totally get that," I say. "They have to pass the vibe check before I'll have any further interaction with someone for personal or professional reasons."

They both stare at me.

"That's a weird way to do business," Harper says.

"You have to be open to people in the work world at least," Mackenzie says, leading the way to a high-top table near the bar.

I take a seat. "In my work, the personal and professional often blur. People hire their friends. That's why I have to be careful. If my gut says something's off, I bail."

"Where's Frankie?" a deep voice says from behind me, startling me.

I turn to see Owen looking grim. "He's, uh…" I look around and find Frankie talking to Jake and Josh near Claire. "With your mom. He does a good job looking after her."

"And who's looking after you?" he asks.

"I'm fine. I'm with people."

"I have a blackbelt." Mackenzie looks around. "Do you think her stalker followed her here?"

"I don't know," Owen snaps. "That's the point. It's not like the doors are locked."

"Chill," Harper says. "It's not that big a place. If something's up, we'll yell. Until then, please leave us in peace. It's a party, and you're bringing everyone down."

Owen glares daggers at Harper, who glares right back. Ah, siblings.

"At least make yourself useful and bring us drinks," Harper says, and then snaps her fingers. "Be quick about it."

His jaw clenches. I'd act as peacemaker, but Owen was acting like a jerk to me earlier, so I just watch.

Mackenzie smooths things over. "I'll get us drinks and, Owen, of course you're welcome to join us. What would everyone like?"

We tell her our order, except Owen, who says, "I need to talk to Frankie."

Mackenzie goes to the bar to put in the drink order.

I give Harper a wry look.

"What?"

"You're purposely trying to make him mad."

She waves that away. "The only way to keep an overbearing older brother in his place is to stand your ground. He was butting in. Obviously, you're fine."

I lean close. "So is this the part where you give me advice about my chances with him?" This was, of course, the entire reason they invited me to the party, and she just drove him away.

"That was Mackenzie's idea," Harper says. "I can tell you right now you don't have a chance with him. He's a wounded bear, and it would take something big, I mean huge, to distract him long enough from his love wound to open up again."

"I apologized. More than once."

"Sometimes sorry's not enough."

My gut churns. I glance across the room, and my gaze collides with his. He's watching me, probably to protect me, not because he's interested. Well, I'm not going to bang my head against the wall. He let me know loud and clear to stay away both in word and action. That's what that jerky behavior was about, a big back-off sign from a wounded bear. I should let him go hibernate and not risk poking the bear again. Enough with the wounded-bear metaphor!

"Where's Mackenzie with our drinks?" I ask.

We both turn toward the bar to see Mackenzie talking to Nathan Brooks, Harper's archnemesis. They grew up together since he lived nearby. I don't know why she can't stand him, only that they were once best friends. When I met him, he was best friends with Owen.

"What's he doing here?" Harper grumbles. "This isn't a work event."

Nathan takes two of the drinks and follows Mackenzie over to us.

"Shit," Harper says under her breath.

"Harper," Nathan says blandly, setting a glass of red wine in front of her.

"Nathan," she says equally blandly. "Thank you for delivering my drink. You remember Shayla."

"Who could forget you." He gives me a warm smile. "Nice of you to slum it with us. I'm sure you have many star-studded invitations."

I smile. "Yes, a lot of work-related obligations, but I love it here. I think it would be awesome to live a safe, quiet life in

Clover Park rather than be hidden away in a hotel room somewhere, always moving with the project."

Mackenzie gives me my margarita and has a mojito for herself. "Nathan was just saying how we need to liven up Clover Park, get more single people to move here. It's mostly families. A great place to grow up, but a little too quiet."

Just then, Owen's aunt Madison taps a microphone for attention. We all look over to see her standing on a chair in the dining area, her husband, Parker, standing by her side. His dark hair is cut short, his jaw clean-shaven. He keeps a hand on her hip, probably to keep her from falling.

Madison looks at her son Michael. "Dad and I just want to say congratulations, Michael. We're so damn proud of you." Her voice cracks, and she shakes her head. "I will *not* cry on such a happy occasion."

Everyone laughs.

"Softie!" Jake yells.

Madison ignores that. "We love you and know you'll do great things."

Everyone cheers and applauds.

Parker helps her down from her chair. Michael walks over to hug his much shorter mom.

Claire takes the microphone and says with a husky laugh, "I'm not going to climb up there, but want to add my congratulations to Michael and also to Rafael. Raf, you followed your heart studying photography, and the art you're creating is beautiful. We're proud to call you son."

Rafael looks visibly moved. "Thanks, Mom."

Harper leans close. "Rafael used to be such a menace with his camera, taking sneak shots of everyone who came over. One time Mom had this uber-famous guy stop by for dinner. Not naming names because it was the classic *movie stars behaving badly* thing. Anyway, he nearly destroyed Rafe's camera when he caught him taking a picture of him. And you know what Rafe did?"

"What?" I whisper.

"He told him he'd never take his picture again, and one

day this guy would wish he would. Rafe was only fourteen too. Talk about confident in his skills."

"You have to tell me who the guy was," I say.

Harper waves that away. I guess I should appreciate her discretion with industry people. I look over just as Rafael's dad, Jake, finishes his speech.

"We wish you all the best in the world, and it's nice to have you home again. Of course, not forever."

Madison pipes up, "I have an awesome move-in-ready house for sale right here in Clover Park."

Jake stares at his sister. "Really, Mad. A sales pitch?"

"I'm the number one real estate agent in the county for a reason," she returns.

Jake goes on to congratulate his dad, Joe, and Brandy on their wedding anniversary. My mind drifts as several people go up to the microphone to share their congratulations. A sense of peace comes over me, one I haven't felt since I was sixteen living with Claire. Maybe it's not Owen I need so much as friends and family right here in Clover Park. Is it possible I'm in love with his family and not him? I brighten, feeling so much better. His family loves me. Why didn't I see this before?

And there's a move-in-ready house in Clover Park. It's driving distance to the city. Mackenzie has an apartment here, and Harper just moved back from Boston and is looking for a place.

As soon as the congratulations announcements end, music starts up from the back room.

"Let's dance," Mackenzie says to us. "Hopefully I'll run into Harry on the way and can test the waters."

Nathan turns to Harper. "Still doing your Kira Stanley moves?" That was a pop singer popular when we were teens.

A rare blush dots Harper's cheeks. "No."

"I'll dance with you," he says. "Make you look good."

"I'd rather dance with a gorilla."

His eyes widen comically. "I don't see any gorillas around here, do you?"

She looks all around before looking at him. "No, just one jackass."

Mackenzie gasps.

"What's your problem with me?" Nathan asks with no heat. Just like he's curious.

Harper's lips press into a flat line. "Nothing. I'm just not one of those women who fall at your feet because you smile or say something supposedly charming."

"Are you jealous?" he asks with a smirk.

"He's single at the moment," Mackenzie puts in.

"Thank you, Mackenzie," Nathan says drily.

"Let's go, ladies," Harper says, leading the way to the back room, where the party seems to have drifted.

I stop her and Mackenzie just before we get to the back room. "I'm having a great time tonight. Let's keep the party going."

Harper gestures ahead to where a bunch of people are dancing and singing to the Neil Diamond song "Sweet Caroline." It's the Boston Red Sox's unofficial anthem. I've seen it on TV during their home games. "The party's still going."

I grab both their hands. "I want to buy that house your aunt mentioned. We can be roommates, and you can live there rent-free."

"Yes!" Harper says. "Let's do it. This is perfect! Now I can save up to buy my own house so much faster." Even though her parents, Claire and Jake, have money, they don't give their kids handouts.

"Should we maybe see the house first?" Mackenzie asks.

"I'll get the details from your aunt, but are you open to it?"

She beams. "Yes."

"Yes?"

She laughs. "Yes!"

We laugh and then launch into a happy dancing hug. This is going to be epic.

9

Owen

"I'm sorry, what?" We're at an outdoor table on Shayla's lunch break, and I can't quite believe my ears. She bought a house in Clover Park, and my sister and cousin are moving in with her? This is a security nightmare.

She puts her fork down. "The important part is, my offer was accepted. Don't worry, it's only a block away from your house, and Madison said a block in the other direction is the police station. The house already has a security system. I just need to transfer it over to me after closing."

I scrub a hand over my face. "Obviously you'll need better than a standard security system, and you still need a body-guard for home and to go to work with you. You can't afford to take risks."

How can I ever relax knowing not only Shayla is at risk, but my family too? Any moment Matt could break in, and who knows what he'll do?

She shows me a picture of an old house on her phone. "It's so beautiful. A restored Victorian with a fenced-in yard. Newly renovated kitchen and baths. And the best part is that it has four bedrooms, so I've got room for Harper, Mackenzie, and my assistant, Olivia."

Shayla looks over at the second-tier craft services with

cold sandwiches, where Olivia is getting her lunch, and waves.

Olivia gestures to see if Shayla needs her, but Shayla waves her off. Olivia goes back to getting her lunch. I met her yesterday when she arrived. She's a no-nonsense brunette, early twenties, with ruthless organization skills. She had Shayla's hotel kitchen set up to mimic her favored foods from her home in LA within an hour before setting up camp in the guest room. She's a film school graduate working to get enough money to produce her own work. One day she'll own Hollywood.

"When did all this happen?" I ask. We live together, and I'm in touch with Mackenzie daily for work. How did I not know a major move was underway?

"It's that house your aunt Madison mentioned at the party on Saturday. I decided to buy it that night, and Harper and Mackenzie agreed to be my roommates."

"So from Saturday to Monday, the house is yours."

"Yup. I offered cash with no contingencies. The owner was eager to move to Florida to be closer to her daughter and grandchildren. We close this Friday and can move in the following Monday. Fortunately, Harper and Mackenzie already have some furniture between them, and Olivia will take care of whatever else we need."

I pinch the top of my nose and close my eyes. *Nightmare.*

"I just love your family," she gushes. "Cooper says he'll stop by to install or fix anything we need. He's fixed lots of stuff at Happy Endings. Mackenzie says he'll eventually take over the restaurant. You're so lucky to have a family who loves to work together and helps each other out."

"So basically you're adopting my family as your own."

She smiles. "Yes. But Claire adopted me as her own first, so I guess it's mutual." She studies my expression. "Why aren't you happy for me?"

I speak through my teeth. "Because that family you love so much, *my family*, is now at risk."

"But you live close by, so maybe you could check in on us regularly."

"Check in on…" I trail off. Obviously, I'll need to move in. I'm not sure if she's hesitant to ask more of me or if she thinks she no longer needs me. Either way, I'm sticking close. Before I can inform her of this, Olivia joins us.

She holds up cookies. "I scored the last pack of Oreos."

"Nice!" Shayla says. Her plate is vegetables with grilled chicken, a side of fruit salad, and sparkling water. Olivia's plate is a sub sandwich, potato chips, Oreos, and Diet Coke.

"You want some of my fruit salad?" Shayla asks.

Olivia takes the bowl and puts the grapes on her plate. "There. Now you don't have to work around them."

"Thank you, Olivia," Shayla says sweetly.

I turn to Olivia, hoping for an ally. "So what do you think of this idea to move to Clover Park and commute into the city?"

Olivia looks to Shayla. "The real answer or the dutiful assistant answer?"

Shayla gestures for her to go on. "I always appreciate your honesty, even if I don't agree with you."

"Right." Olivia turns to me. "It's a logistical nightmare. We're going to have to be up at five a.m. to drive in for makeup and hair call time, returning in what will likely be rush-hour traffic back home. I've suggested using the house for weekends only."

"But that won't make it feel like a home," Shayla says. "I want to be part of daily life there with you, Mackenzie, and Harper. Having dinner together, binge-watching TV, catching up on our lives. Maybe I'll even get a cat."

"No cat," Olivia says. "I draw the line at a cat. I'm allergic."

"What about a hairless cat?" Shayla asks. At Olivia's pointed look, Shayla says sheepishly, "Okay, no cat."

Who's the boss of who here?

"And what happens when you go off for your next job?" I

ask. "Harper and Mackenzie are on the hook for the mortgage payment?"

Shayla stares at me. "What kind of friend do you think I am? Of course not. I paid for the house in full, and they can live there rent-free for as long as they want. I'll come back to live there when I'm between jobs."

"She's keeping the house in LA too," Olivia says. "It's important to have a homebase there."

Right. My parents still keep an LA house for when they're out there. Seems like Shayla's following in Mom's footsteps with a Connecticut homebase and an LA house. Still, I'm not happy.

"You can't live there without a guard," I say.

"I'm on it," Olivia says. "I've got three candidates lined up for Shayla to meet in person this week." She tilts her head at me. "For the vibe check."

"Right, the vibe check." I'm a temporary part of her life. I have to remember that.

I give Shayla a hard look. "I've got my work cut out for me, securing an old Victorian, making sure you and my family are safe. And you too, Olivia."

"Don't worry about me," she says before taking a bite of sub. She's short and round, kind of an apple shape. I can't see her taking down a stalker.

"Why shouldn't I worry?" I ask. "Do you have self-defense training?"

"If I ever see Matt Boone in person, I'll kick him in the balls," Olivia says matter-of-factly. "I always wear steel-toed boots."

I look under the table. Yup, black steel-toed boots with a white belted dress. She's starting to remind me of my aunt Madison. Badass to the bone despite their petite size.

I spread my arms wide. "Sounds like you ladies have it all under control."

Shayla beams.

"He's being sarcastic," Olivia whispers.

"I like you," I say to Olivia.

"Thank you."

Shayla frowns. "I know you're worried, but it'll all be fine, and I'll be out of your hair." She lifts her chin, her eyes glittering. "I'm sorry I got you involved in the first place. I'll have everything I've ever wanted in my new home in Clover Park."

I stiffen. Guess she was just acting when she talked about missing me or that I was the best she ever had.

"Well, I'm sorry you ever came back," I snap. "How am I supposed to sleep at night knowing you've put my family in danger?"

Shayla's face crumples.

My gut churns. "I didn't mean—" I start.

She looks away, her voice a whisper. "You should go."

I walk a distance away. Not too far, I need to keep watch. Dammit, why does Shayla have to make everything so damn complicated?

Shayla

I'm so excited to tour the house with Mackenzie and Harper. It's officially ours. We're here on a Saturday morning to measure the spaces and decide what we need. Olivia is here, too, to keep a running list of stuff to buy.

"Aunt Mad was right," Mackenzie says. "It's definitely move-in ready. The hardwood floors look recently redone. Look at the crown molding in the living room!"

We're in the front parlor room with a large fireplace and have a view of the formal living room through an archway. To the left is a dining room and, just beyond that, a kitchen.

Harper, Olivia, and I follow Mackenzie into the living room. Owen skulks behind us. He's not happy with me for buying a house to live in with my friends, who happen to be his family members. I'm not putting them at risk. I planned on having a guard and a good security system. But no-o-o, Owen rejected my choice in bodyguard, saying he was too inexperienced, even though Owen didn't have any bodyguard experience until recently. I thought JJ had plenty of experience after five years with a famous family. Anyway, Owen's staying on an extra week while Olivia finds another candidate.

I set Owen free, and he refused to go. Yesterday was supposed to be his last day. Now he acts like I'm forcing him to be here when he was the one who rejected his replacement. *Door's right there, Mr. Grumpy!*

"I can just picture a sofa, love seat, and ottoman in here," Mackenzie says. "Maybe some antique tables."

"That would be in keeping with the period, but I thought we'd be more modern casual," I say.

"Exactly," Harper says. "I have a great red velvet sofa for this room."

"I have a brown leather sofa," Mackenzie says. "One can go in the parlor and one in the living room. I think the TV should go in here."

Owen walks over to the back window to look at the yard with its six-foot-tall privacy fence. Even he has to agree it's a nice private spot. There's a vegetable garden with fencing around it to keep out the wildlife, a small fountain, and a large patio. I love it.

"Let's talk kitchen supplies," Olivia says, heading toward the kitchen with a clipboard, a pen tucked behind her ear. I'm so lucky to have her on my team.

We follow her. The kitchen is done all in white—white cabinets, white counters, white sinks, white tile floors. Silver accents on the cabinet handles and drawer pulls, along with stainless-steel appliances, stand out in contrast.

"They did a nice job on the renovation," I say. "Madison showed me the original blueprint, and the kitchen used to be half this size. They expanded it farther into the back and added on the powder room and laundry room at the same time. They also made the living room bigger and added the bay window."

"This is a dream kitchen," Harper says. "Too bad I don't cook."

"I can make omelets and stir-fries," I offer.

"I can bake desserts and make bread," Mackenzie says. "Mostly carbs."

"Hello, hello," a warm masculine voice calls.

I step into the small foyer to find Mackenzie's younger brother Cooper wearing a toolbelt over faded jeans.

"Ready to help," he says with a smile. He's grown into his formerly lanky frame—six feet, muscular and athletic like all the Campbell men. Now why couldn't I be hung up on a sweet guy like him? Unfortunately, he's two years younger, and I'll forever see him as Mackenzie's little brother who used to run wild and throw food at us. Now that he's in his twenties, he's much calmer.

I smile. "Hey, Cooper. Come take the tour with us. We're trying to figure out what we need before move-in tomorrow."

Owen appears by my side. "You left the front door unlocked?"

"It's not like we're living here yet. We're just scoping the place out. Besides, you're with me."

Cooper gives Owen a handshake with a slap on the back.

"Cooper to the rescue again," Owen says.

"What do you mean?" I ask.

Owen points to him. "Cooper rescues women. It's his thing."

Cooper scoffs. "It's not my *thing*. I'm just helpful."

I smile at Cooper. What a sweetheart. "Well, we don't need rescuing, but I sure do appreciate you being here to take a look around. There's some damaged plaster in my room, and I would love some shelving in my closet. Right now there's just a single rod."

"I'll take a look," he says. "Which room?"

"Last one on the right."

He jogs up the stairs.

Owen gives me a sour look before heading to the front

door and locking it. "We need better locks for this and the back door."

"I trust your judgment," I say cheerfully before joining my new roommates.

A short while later, everyone's upstairs, inspecting every bedroom, bathroom, and closet. We've each claimed a bedroom. Harper has a new job in the city, but only goes in twice a week. She works from home the other days. Mackenzie says she also works from home unless they have a team meeting or she just wants a change of scenery.

Mackenzie looks out the upstairs window of her room. "So when's the B&B supposed to open across the street?"

I join her, admiring the old Victorian. Owen stands in the doorway behind us. "Not for a while. Madison says the house was inherited and the estate settled, but the owner is still waiting on a permit to make it a B&B. Apparently, it was her grandmother's place."

"That's Maggie O'Hare's old house," Mackenzie says. "She's a legend. Talk about someone who knew everyone and everything going on in town. She lived to be a hundred and wore leopard bodysuits and leather pants to the end. That's how I want to be at that age."

"Senior goals," I say.

We laugh.

Owen joins us. "How am I just now hearing about a B&B across the street? This is not good. Matt could legit check in as a guest and blend right in."

"Wouldn't that be violating his restraining order?" I ask.

"It's more than one hundred yards away." He pinches the top of his nose, closing his eyes.

"It's okay, Owen," Mackenzie says. "By the time the permits go through and they finish renovating, Shayla will be on to her next project."

"But she said this would be her home base," Owen says.

"That's so sweet, Shay!" Mackenzie says. "I thought this would be more like your vacation house."

"It's not sweet," Owen says. "It's insane, and she's putting all of you at risk."

I ignore him. "You're family," I tell Mackenzie. "At least I hope so. I don't really have any family anymore."

Mackenzie wraps an arm around me. "Of course we are. Harper! Get in here. Shayla's getting all mushy, and you've got to get in on a group hug."

Owen rolls his eyes.

Harper rushes in a moment later and nearly tackles us in a hug. We stumble and laugh.

"Why're we mushy?" Harper asks.

"I said this would be my home base because you guys are family," I say.

"We have to adopt her," Mackenzie says. "You're officially my sister. I always wanted a sister."

"Me too," Harper says.

"Me three," I say over the lump of emotion lodged in my throat. "I'm so happy."

Ding-dong. We pull apart at the sound of the doorbell. Goosebumps rise on my arms. We were only expecting Cooper.

I rush to reassure my new sisters. "Matt wouldn't ring the bell."

"We're not bending our life around one sad little stalker man," Harper says. "After we've taken precautions, I say we go about life as usual."

Ding-dong.

Mackenzie gestures toward the door. "It could be Finn. I asked him to stop by to talk about painting some of the interior rooms. He's looking to make some extra money to buy a car." Finn is her youngest brother.

Ding-dong.

Part of me wants Owen to go downstairs and answer the door, but I know he's not our butler.

I try to sound cheery despite my fear. "It sounds so official, like this is a real home with a real doorbell."

"Of course it's a real home," Harper says.

"Maybe we could change it so it's more of a chime than a ding-dong," Mackenzie says.

"I'll get the door," Olivia announces from the hallway.

Owen follows her. "Look through the peephole before opening it."

Mackenzie heads downstairs. "Finn!"

Harper and I follow. Finn's resemblance to Mackenzie and Cooper is clear, same dark hair and angular cheekbones. He has blue eyes like Mackenzie. He's nineteen, on break from college. I caught up with him at the party last weekend.

"Saw Cooper's car out front," Finn says to Mackenzie. "You paying him too?"

"Shh," Mackenzie says. "He volunteered to fix stuff. You get paid because I know you're a poor college student."

He pulls a flip book from his back jeans pocket. "I brought paint samples. Just let me know what you want."

Olivia holds out her palm. "I'll take that since I'll be doing the ordering. We want to keep things neutral for the eclectic collection of furniture coming in here." She studies her clipboard. "Some very different styles merging with this move."

Finn stares at her, his jaw slack. Like he's starstruck, only Olivia isn't famous.

"Can I have the paint samples?" Olivia prompts.

"I'm Finn Campbell," he says, offering his hand.

She shakes it firmly. "Olivia Wagner. I'm Shayla's assistant." She takes the paint sample book from his other hand.

"She's so much more than an assistant," I say. "She's a genius life organizer. And a graduate of film school."

"Cool," Finn says. "I live about four blocks from here if you ever want to get a drink."

Mackenzie titters. "Finnie, she's closer to my age. You're still a teenager."

"So?" Finn says. "I'm an adult."

Olivia smooths her hair and sends me a *can you believe this* look. As a rule, men don't ask Olivia out for drinks. In fact, I don't think she's dated since college, which is a shame because she's cute and brilliant. Today she's wearing a baggy short-sleeved shirt over leggings with her standard black steel-toed boots. Okay, so she's not a fashionista, but she has many fine qualities. I'm glad Finn sees past her weekend outfit.

Finn moves closer to talk to Olivia, pointing out some colors in the paint sample book. He looks at her profile often, seeming to admire her. She studies the paint colors, oblivious to his attention.

I gesture for everyone to join me in the living room to give them some space. Once we're all in the room, Mackenzie whispers, "I've never seen Finn look like that before. Like he was struck by lightning the moment he saw her."

"Love goggled," Harper says way too loud.

"It's sweet," I whisper. "She's only four years older than him."

"That's a lot at Finn's age," Mackenzie says. "He asked her out for drinks, and he can't even legally buy a drink yet."

"So they'll get coffee," I say.

"Or she can buy him a drink," Harper says.

I peek into the foyer to see Finn flirting with Olivia, all smiles and husky voice. Olivia shakes her head. Maybe I should intervene. She's not used to rejecting men, and this one must be handled gently. He's going to be around a lot, painting the interior.

I walk toward the foyer with Owen close on my heels. I glance over my shoulder at him, and he gestures for me to keep going.

I arrive just in time to hear Olivia say, "Nothing personal, you're just too young for me."

Finn's gaze is intent on hers. "I'm going to marry you one day, Olivia Wagner."

My jaw gapes. Owen proposed to me at seventeen, and now Finn proposes at nineteen. What's with the men in this family leaping to a commitment? At least Owen and I were in love. Finn just met her.

Olivia stares at him. "No, you're not."

"Yes, I am. Mark my words."

She crosses her arms. "I won't be working for Shayla forever, you know. At some point I'm moving back to LA, and one day I'll run my own studio."

He grins. "We'll stay in touch." He swaggers away.

She stares after him and then turns back to me. "What's his deal?"

"That was strange even for him," Owen says.

"He's way into you," I say.

She scoffs. "Guys who look like that are never into me." She shakes her head. "There must be another reason. Maybe he's trying to go through me to get to you."

We all look over at Finn, where Mackenzie is busy lecturing him in big-sister mode. He looks over to Olivia and winks.

She gasps. "We need a new painter. I'll start looking right away."

"You can't fire him just for asking you out," I say. "Besides, he's trying to earn money for a car."

"I'll talk to him," Owen says. "I'll let him know you're not interested, so no flirting."

"And no winking," Olivia says, straightening her shirt. "No funny business."

"Got it." Owen heads over to Finn.

I give Olivia's arm a squeeze. "Wait 'til you meet the rest of the family. Owen's got a brother and several single cousins of eligible age. Maybe you'll hit it off with one of them."

She frowns. "I don't have time for dating."

"Are you happy, Olivia?"

"What's happiness got to do with anything? This is work."

I decide not to push it. I should just be glad she's so focused on the work I need her to do. "I so appreciate you."

She writes something on the paper on her clipboard. "As you should."

I nudge her shoulder.

"Thank you," she says with a small smile and heads upstairs.

Owen returns to me. "Finn says he won't flirt if she doesn't want him to, but he's still convinced there's something between them. I think he inherited his mom's romantic nature. Poor bastard." Finn's mom is Hailey, the wedding planner and self-proclaimed love junkie.

"He'll make some woman very happy one day," I say.

Owen grunts. "I know move-in day is tomorrow, but you can't stay here until I've got the whole place secured. You'll need to stay at the hotel another night. It should be ready by Monday night or Tuesday night at the latest."

"I'm not missing my first night with my honorary sisters," I say.

He clenches his jaw. He does that a lot around me. "You hired me to do a job, and that's what I'm doing."

"It's been more than a week since Matt's done anything. Maybe he's moved on."

He lets out a breath. "That's wishful thinking."

I rub my temple. He's not wrong.

"If you insist on staying here, then I'm staying here too," he says.

I brighten, the words tumbling out rapid-fire. "Why didn't you say so? You can sleep on the couch downstairs. I'd love that. I was going to ask you anyway. It makes the most sense, and actually, I thought that might've been your intention all along since you rejected the bodyguard we were going to hire. Which is fine since we have you."

"Fine."

"Great! And then I'll hire a new guard, and you can go back to your work."

"Absolutely. Mackenzie says things are moving forward with the DC project. It's going to the next level of committee for review."

"Good for you."

I run out of steam and just look at him mutely, glad he's sticking around. His eyes are intent on mine, and something shifts in that moment. A tension shimmering in the air between us. It's not angry. It's more…potential.

I take his hand and give it a squeeze. "I'm really glad you're here. I hope—" My voice catches as he leans down, his lips mere millimeters from mine. My heart hammers, my breath quickening. It's happening. It's finally happening.

He eases closer still, our breaths mingling. My eyes close, my entire body vibrating in anticipation. I sway toward him; the heat between us is palpable. Finally, he's—

Gone.

I open my eyes to find he's backed off.

He smirks. "I know why you really moved to town." He swaggers over to Cooper.

I scowl. Faking me out with an almost kiss!

I want to yell it wasn't because of you! But there're too many witnesses to give in to a fit of temper. I'm here for my friends and to feel normal for once. Living the small-town life in Clover Park is exactly what I need.

Someone needs a dose of reality.

10

———

It's move-in day! I stand on the front porch and direct some movers to where a rug should go. It's really happening. I'm going to have a real home with friends who're like family. Unlike my lonely house in LA or the many temporary hotel rooms I call home.

I let out a happy sigh, turn, and freeze. There's a beige car parked across the street, and the man inside stares directly at me. My heart's in my throat. He's wearing a hat and sunglasses, so I can't see him clearly, but the intensity of his stare tells me it's Matt.

Olivia comes out. "Your bedroom is set up. Do you want to take a look at the furniture arrangement? I think—Shayla? Why are you frozen like a statue?"

"That man," I say under my breath.

She texts while talking to me at the same time. "I can't tell from here. Is it Matt or a pap?"

"Matt."

"Let's go inside."

I turn to go and nearly collide with Owen. He tells Olivia to get me inside, takes a picture of the guy, and strides across the street.

I go to the front room, my legs shaky as I lower myself to Harper's soft velvet sofa. Olivia rushes to the kitchen and returns with a plastic cup of water. She brought paper plates, plastic cups, and plastic silverware for us to use until we could get unpacked. She thinks of everything.

I take the water with a shaking hand and drink until it's gone. Then I close my eyes and focus on breathing.

"We don't know who it was yet," Olivia says. "No need to panic."

"I'm not panicking. I'm breathing to prevent panic from setting in."

She sits next to me. "I'll breathe too."

After a few moments, I open my eyes. Reality crashes in on me. "I've been in serious denial about moving here, dreaming I could have a normal small-town life. Now I've brought this horrible person to our door."

Harper walks in with a lamp. "What horrible person?"

I swallow hard. "There's a man across the street in a beige car, watching the house. I think it's Matt."

"Oh, I wondered who Owen was talking to. That guy took off."

Owen walks in a moment later. "I got his picture and his license plate, so I can let the local police know who to look for. That was Matt. He followed us here from the city."

"I'm sorry," I say in a small voice.

His entire demeanor changes, from tough to concerned. "Hey, it's not your fault." He sits by my side, wraps an arm around my shoulders, and pulls me in close. Tears threaten. For so long I've longed to be in his arms again, feeling safe and protected from the world. Just not under these circumstances.

Olivia slips away.

He tips my chin up. "I'll never let anything happen to you. You're too important."

"To you?"

He gazes into my eyes. "To everyone."

"Owen." *Be real with me.*

"You know what you are to me," he says gruffly.

"I don't."

"You're different. Special."

I hug him, tears stinging my eyes. He's not as closed off as I feared. Maybe it took a threat for him to realize what I meant to him.

I pull back and meet his eyes. He strokes my cheek and gives me a tender kiss. I wrap my arms around his neck and return the kiss with all the pent-up feeling I have for my one and only love.

"At least pick a room," Harper says.

We break apart as she walks past on her way to the moving truck outside.

Owen rubs the back of his neck. "We probably shouldn't do that again. I need to keep some professional distance to be a good guard."

"But wouldn't I be safer pressed close against you?"

He runs a finger down my nose. "Getting close to me is never a safe thing."

"I don't believe that."

He shifts away. "Back to the Matt situation. I told him he was looking at jail time if he showed up here again."

"And that made him leave?"

"Yeah. Worked like a charm. Well, first I took off his sunglasses, told him to look me in the eye and understand that if I ever see him again, I'll haul him to jail faster than he can say restraining order."

"Wow. And then he took off?"

"Not yet. I took his picture while he glared at me, and then I crushed his expensive sunglasses under my foot, he cursed a blue streak, and *then* he took off."

I wring my hands together. "But what if he sells that story to a gossip rag? I mean, that you threatened him. It'll be all over the internet."

"He's not going to sell a story that implicates him in stalking, especially with the restraining order. Anyway, he started panicking when I mentioned jail and the police, saying he lived here, and when I called him on the lie, he started yelling that he pays taxes."

My eyes widen. "He sounds crazy."

"Yup."

"Do you think he'll be back?"

"Depends how determined he is."

"Can I see his picture?"

He shows me his phone.

The hair on the back of my neck stands on end. That's him. And unlike when I see him trying to be charming to lure me in, in this picture he looks like the frustrated angry man he is.

"I'm scared," I admit.

"You should be."

"Oh God, I've put Harper and Mackenzie in terrible danger."

He exhales sharply. "So now you finally listen to reason after you've bought the place and moved in."

I stand. "I have to talk to them."

I find them upstairs in Mackenzie's room, setting a mirror over the dresser. "I'm thinking of moving out."

"What! Already?" Mackenzie says.

"Matt showed up across the street. Now that he knows I'm here, I feel like I'm putting you both at risk."

Harper pipes up, "Hey, we knew the risk of living with an A-list star. I grew up with one."

"Yeah," Mackenzie says. "Besides, Owen's rigging the place with the best security, and he lives close by. He'll be with us until your new guard starts, right?"

I let out a shaky breath. "Yes."

"There you go," Mackenzie says. "And the police are just a block away."

Owen appears in the doorway.

Harper plants her hands on her hips. "I just heard you're sticking around a little longer. How am I supposed to enjoy the orgy with big brother here?"

Owen makes a face of disgust and leaves. Harper grins.

∽

After a dinner of takeout from Happy Endings, a shared bottle of wine, and a lot of talking and laughing, we all settle in for the night.

I stretch out in bed and close my eyes. Olivia is next door to me, Harper and Mackenzie across the hall, and Owen downstairs keeping watch. He gave us space tonight, staying to himself in the kitchen with his laptop. Just knowing he's here makes me feel better.

I review all the ways I'm safe. The police are close by. I'm living with other people and a man who's trained and fearless.

It's not enough.

Anxiety creeps in. How hard would it be to get to me? What if Matt climbed to my window? What if he somehow snuck past a sleeping Owen?

What if Matt has a gun? My heart races. Owen doesn't carry one. He'd need a permit and a mandatory training class, and since he was just standing in temporarily, he didn't follow through with that.

I turn on the light on my nightstand, grab my phone, and text Owen.

Me: *Can you come upstairs?*

Owen: *What's wrong?*

Me: *I had a nightmare.*

A living nightmare, my real life. I scramble out of bed and open the door slowly so it doesn't creak and alert the others that I have a visitor.

A moment later, he slips inside. He's in a T-shirt and jogging pants. How bad is it that I was hoping he'd be shirtless? Even in these scary circumstances, I still lust after Owen. There must be something wrong with me.

"You're safe," he says, shutting the door behind him and locking it. "I'm sure I scared him enough to stay away for at least a day."

"Stay with me tonight. At least until I'm asleep. Please."

He blows out a breath. "This is why I said to stay at the hotel." He checks the window lock.

"I know, I'm sorry. Please stay."

He turns and takes in my pajamas. "Are those the same pajamas from nine years ago? That shirt's been washed so many times it's as thin as tissue."

"So? I like it that way." I run my hands down the thin cotton of my Tweety bird pajama top. "It's comfortable."

He gestures toward my chest in a jerky motion. "I can see right through your shirt. You weren't wearing that downstairs earlier." He sounds accusatory like I'm wearing it to seduce him.

"Owen, if I wanted to seduce you, I'd have answered the door naked. I'm scared and just want you close."

I turn and get into bed, holding the covers out to him.

He stares at the bed for a long moment, grumbles something to himself, and joins me.

I turn off the light on my nightstand and cuddle up to him, pressing my face into his chest and throwing an arm around his big heated body. "Mmm, this was exactly what I needed."

He cups my head with his hand, and I sigh, relaxing into him.

His voice rumbles in his chest. "I remember these pajamas the first night you stayed with us."

I look up at him. "I remember what you were wearing too. Jogging pants with no shirt. Harper yelled at you to stop showing off your muscles."

He chuckles. "That was the year I started working out with weights. I was shirtless in front of girls as much as possible."

His fingers run through my hair, soothing me.

"Owen, I missed this. I missed you."

"Shay." His voice sounds strained. He wants me as much as I want him.

I'm not sure who moves first, but we're suddenly kissing in a passionate frenzy. His hands are all over me. I tug at his shirt, and he sits up to pull it off; then he pulls me up, lifting off my shirt.

He turns on the light on the nightstand. "Just as beautiful as I remember."

I run my palms over the ridges of muscle on his chest and abs. "You too, only much more muscled."

He lowers me to the mattress and covers me, kissing along my neck, nipping and sucking as he works his way down my body.

I gasp as his mouth reaches my breast and suckles while he caresses my other breast. He switches sides, and my back arches, seeking more. I run my fingers through the soft hair curling at the nape of his neck, a familiarity in the gesture merging passionate memories with now.

He lowers himself down my body, yanks my shorts down, and stares at my pink thong. "This is new," he croaks.

"I did buy new underwear in the last nine years."

He runs his finger along the line of the thong, bringing a rush of desire. Then he peels off the thong and slowly lowers his head. I hold my breath. He kisses along the crease of my thigh as his fingers stroke me expertly. My hips rock, begging for more.

I gasp as his lips press against the magic spot, and then his tongue. My eyes roll back in my head. He's picked up some moves, and I'm not complaining. Pleasure rolls through me in waves as his lips and tongue and, oh, God, those questing fingers take over my body.

My fingers curl into the sheets. He pushes on relentlessly as my insides coil and tighten. "Oh my God, Owen! I'm—"

His fingers thrust in my mouth, silencing me. I suck eagerly, unable to contain all that I'm feeling. He's making me crazed with that hungry mouth of his. My hips buck, and his fingers leave my mouth to pin my hips to the mattress.

He lifts his head. "Shhh!"

"Don't stop," I beg.

He lowers his head, pushing me once again to the edge. I cry out as the orgasm hits hard, my entire body shuddering with ecstasy. His mouth covers mine, swallowing my sounds of pleasure, even as he strokes me gently, letting me ride out every last wave. Finally, I go limp.

He lifts his head to look at me. "You can't be that loud with my sister and cousin across the hall."

"You made me."

He grins. "I did, didn't I?"

"Come inside me," I whisper.

He groans. "Condom."

"Yes. Olivia always puts some nearby for me." I reach for the nightstand drawer, but he beats me to it.

"Of course she does," he grumbles. He grabs one and rolls it on. Then he pins my hands to the mattress. "Now keep the noise level down."

He thrusts inside me, and we both groan.

"Shh," I whisper in his ear, wrapping my legs high around his waist and lifting my hips to take him deeper.

"You feel so damn good," he says in my ear.

And then there's no more talking. Just a primal joining of two bodies meant for each other. Nothing but the sound of his harsh breath as he thrusts over and over. He lifts my hips, his next thrust hitting the G spot. I chant his name until he covers my mouth with his, his tongue thrusting inside. I'm filled with him, overwhelmed, and I let go, the release rocketing through me.

He lifts his head and lets out a guttural groan as he goes over with me. He collapses on top of me, stealing my breath. A moment later, he rolls to his back, tucking me against his side.

We're quiet, catching our breath.

After a few moments, he says, "You have to move in with me. It's the safest option."

I prop up on an elbow to look at him. "Is it really about safety?"

"I want you close, okay?"

"Because…"

He sighs. "Because I care about you. You know that."

I bite back a smile. He acts like his feelings have been

obvious all this time. He's done a good job of hiding them behind a grumpy exterior.

"This is the sex talking just like the first time when you proposed after sex," I say in a teasing voice.

"I was seventeen. Of course I proposed. I was so excited to be having sex. That didn't mean anything."

Hurt has me drawing back. I turn off the light and settle in bed flat on my back.

He hauls me sideways against him, drawing my arm and leg across him.

I huff. "Manhandle me more, why don't you?"

He chuckles. "Don't mind if I do."

"I'm not living with you. I just bought this place."

"One, you need to for peace of mind, mine and yours. I need to know you're safe and that my cousin and sister aren't at risk."

Guilt stabs at me. I was in serious denial about moving here. "What's two?"

He kisses me and nips my bottom lip. "You're too damn noisy to keep this up with them right across the hall."

"What makes you think we're going to keep this up?"

He slides his fingers between my legs, stoking fresh desire. I clamp my mouth against the moan that threatens to escape. He slips his fingers inside, unerringly finding the spot that sets me off. The breath whooshes from my lungs.

I rock helplessly against him as he pushes me on and on, white-hot pleasure arcing through my body.

"Tell me you want me to stop," he whispers in my ear.

I can't speak, my nails digging into his shoulders, and then he stops.

"Don't stop, never stop," I say.

He gives me a sexy smile. "This is why you need to move in with me."

"You play dirty."

His questing fingers return, drawing me to the edge of release and holding me there. I tremble at the brink. All I can do is cling to his shoulders as he takes over, amping up the pleasure and pausing just long enough to amp it up further.

I whimper incoherently, passion clouding my vision. And then an explosion of pleasure hits so hard I scream. His mouth's on mine instantly, swallowing my cries of pleasure as he rocks me slowly, gently back to stillness.

He eases to his back and drapes my limp body over him, spreading my legs so I can still feel every nerve on fire. I'm too spent to move.

He pulls the covers over us and cups my head to his chest. "We definitely need privacy, my little screamer."

"Your fault," I murmur and fall asleep in a sensual haze.

I wake before dawn to a fully aroused male spooning me from behind, his fingers already readying me for more. "Owen," I half moan.

He pulls my leg back over his and takes me in one hard thrust. I gasp and then pant as he pushes me beyond every limit I thought pleasure had. By the time he's finished with me, I'm his. There will never be another like him.

Afterwards, he slides me to my stomach and takes his time massaging me from my scalp to my toes. I sigh into the mattress. He lifts my hips, and it begins again. He can't get enough of me, taking all I have to give, and then taking more.

I surrender to the pleasure, to him. This was a long time coming.

11

———

I'm up early for Shayla's call time after a fantastic night and early morning too. I walk into the kitchen for coffee, tired but extremely relaxed. I convinced her to move in with me, so I don't have to worry about any danger coming to my sister or cousin by association. All I have to do is keep things casual and light. Last night was fun, and we can have more fun too.

Okay, it was more than great sex. It was like we picked up where we left off, both of us crazy about each other. She has this way of touching me, a way of looking at me that feels like—

What have I done?

I exhale sharply. It's fine. Nothing to worry about. Shayla will move on eventually like she always does. I know the score. This is temporary. Why shouldn't I enjoy myself? As long as I'm careful not to let her all the way in. No big expectations, so no one gets hurt.

Harper walks in. "Did you hear those weird sounds last night? Sounded like a dying animal. Maybe a coyote took down a deer in the backyard."

I pour coffee into my travel mug. "I didn't hear anything." She's talking about Shayla's sex sounds. It's too early to deal with shit from my sister.

"What're you doing up so early?" I ask.

"Shay said I could ride into the city with you guys for work today. Saves me time going the train route."

"She's moving in with me tonight."

"No, she's not." She pours herself a cup of coffee and looks in the refrigerator, pulling out a yogurt.

"Yes, she is. She agreed last night."

"During the deer attack?"

"Ha-ha. Ask her yourself."

"Ask me what?" Shayla says, walking in with her hair wet and piled on top of her head. She's wearing a loose T-shirt and jogging pants. Nothing about this picture should be enticing, but I'm instantly hard.

I shift toward the counter, covering the evidence and fiddling with the lid of my travel mug. "You're moving in with me tonight. Harper doesn't believe me."

Shayla pours coffee into her travel mug. "Oh, well, I'm not sure if that's the right way to go. It's like a fast-forward for a relationship that's only just begun."

I shift to face her. *A relationship? Are you sticking around? Because that's the only way I'd take that risk.*

Harper pounces. "Ooh, a relationship? I didn't know that's what was going on. Since when?"

"It just happened last night," Shayla says, sending me a warm smile.

I look from her to Harper. It's way too early to be having this conversation. The sun didn't even come up yet. And, obviously, I'm not going there in front of my sister.

"I'm going to get ready," I say and walk out at a quick pace, but not too quick. I don't want to hurt Shay's feelings.

Harper's voice carries out to the hallway. "Nothing scares a guy away faster than bringing up the relationship."

I don't wait around to hear Shayla's response to that.

❧

That night I sit on Shayla's bed and watch her pack a suitcase. I convinced her at lunch that her moving in with me was best for everyone's safety. She was suitably worried about her friends to oblige. I'm more relieved than I'd like to admit. Truth is, I can't bear any harm coming to her or, God forbid, to lose her because of some crazy stalker. No. Not on my watch.

"Mackenzie and Harper weren't too happy with you moving out," I say.

She nods. "At least Nathan put in the top-of-the-line security system today. Even so, I know it's for the best that I leave. I'm the big draw for the crazy."

"It won't always be like this. You just have to be super cautious right now."

"I should've listened to you in the first place. Safety first." She comes over and gives me a soft kiss. "I'm just so happy you forgave me."

Did I forgive her?

"What's there to forgive?"

"You know, me not staying in touch, especially after you proposed to me."

"We were kids."

"True, but the love was real. And you just asked me to live with you."

"Yeah, but that's not permanent, right? You'll go wherever—"

"Vancouver. Ooh, Owen. You should come with me. I can get you a security gig with the studio. Spotlight Pictures is an indie studio, but they're up and coming and very well regarded. There's always expensive equipment that needs to be secured, not to mention the talent. It would be a whole new market for you. Would you like that?"

Mackenzie talked about getting a foot in the door with Hollywood before when she wanted me to take the job with Shayla. No doubt it could be very lucrative. Not only do they have expensive sets and equipment, they often want to keep the movie under wraps until just before launch. I'd have to give up the DC job or postpone it until Nathan could take over. Assuming we get it. Mackenzie thinks we will.

"Think about it, okay?" she says, stroking my beard and kissing me again.

I flop backwards on her bed, staring at the ceiling. Things are going at lightning speed. Within weeks I could be in a new business venture, staying with Shayla on location in Vancouver, living with her, in a relationship. Me, the die-hard bachelor sworn to keep my heart under wraps because of the damage she did to it in the first place!

Somebody has to slam on the brakes!

"Shay, this thing between us, it's more casual, you know?"

Her dresser drawer slams shut. "What do you mean?"

"I mean this is way too fast. I can't be following you around from set to set, even if I can get work out of it."

She stands next to the bed, staring down at me. "Why not?"

"Because I have my own life here."

She sits next to me. "We can make Clover Park our home-base, so you'd still see all your friends and family regularly."

I sit up and stare straight ahead, steeling myself against tears. Hers, not mine. "I'm just saying I saw this thing between us as more casual, you know?"

"You invited me to live with you."

I turn to her. "For my sanity. I can't stand knowing Harper and Mackenzie are at risk if Matt comes back."

"That's the only reason?"

"And because you're noisy in bed." It's all true, but it's not the whole truth. I'm backpedaling because she expects me to drop my life for hers, and that's never going to happen. There's no real future for us.

She huffs. "Well, you don't have to worry about that anymore." She grabs her suitcase and dumps the contents on the bed.

I grab her by the waist and pull her into my lap, wrapping my arms around her. She pushes at my chest for a moment and then gives up, scowling at me.

"You're giving me very mixed messages," she says. "No relationship, move in with me, and now you're hugging me."

"Can't we just live together casually?"

"No."

"Why not?"

"Because that is not a thing. I've never lived with a guy before, but you asked, and after your convincing argument, I decided yes." She places her hand on my jaw and gazes into my eyes. "I never got over you."

"But you were with—"

"No one ever meant as much to me as you did." She rubs my chest. "So we good? I move in for our relationship, and you go to Vancouver with me for work? I'm sure I can pull some strings and make a job happen for you."

The old hurts come rushing back. "How was I supposed to know you never got over me? You kept in touch with everyone but me. I had to hear from Mom, Harper, and Mackenzie how great you were doing. You even invited them to visit and not me."

"Because you were more important than any of them!"

"That doesn't make sense."

"Okay, hypothetically, if I'd invited you to visit, then what? You'd ultimately have to go home for school or college or, I don't know, your life. It would've hurt both of us to get together and separate over and over and over. But now we're in a different place in our lives."

I'm quiet, unsure if I'm willing to pick up where we left off. It's only been two weeks since she crashed into my life!

She cups my face in her hands. "When my bodyguard quit, the first person I thought of was you. I realized I'd never really let you go, and I hoped this was an opportunity to see if there was still something there between us. And there is."

I pull away from her. "I get it. You're lonely, you can't trust guys you meet in the industry, so you go back to your summer fling and try to make something happen. I have a life, and you can't just expect me to drop everything to fit into yours."

I walk out.

"Where're you going?" she yells down the hallway.

I stop and turn around. "Back to our original arrangement. I'll be on the couch. Tell Olivia she has until the end of the week to find a replacement for me."

"What about Harper and Mackenzie's safety?" she asks.

"You should've thought of that before you dragged them into this."

I march downstairs, pissed at the way Shayla's turning my life upside down and for what? Nostalgia? I'm still not happy about Harper and Mackenzie living with her either, but they knew the risk as well as Shayla. It's time I stop playing big brother, stop trying to protect everyone. We're all adults here.

I can't wait to get back to my real job.

Shayla

I scoot back against the cushioned headboard next to Mackenzie. We're in her room. Harper's sitting cross-legged on the end of the bed. I've just shared the whole Owen story with them.

"So temperamental," Harper says. "And they say women are the emotional ones. Ha!"

"He never got over you," Mackenzie says.

"Oh, he's over me."

"*Brrap!*" Harper makes a game-show buzzer sound for wrong answer. "Sorry, try again."

"He proposed the night before I left that summer," I say. "I never told you that."

"Oh my God, what did you say?" Harper asks.

I lift my palms. "Nothing. I didn't have an answer at sixteen."

Mackenzie turns to me. "To be fair, it's pretty quick to invite him to move with you to Vancouver after one night of animal sex."

Harper snorts. "True. By the way, you sound like a dying deer. I told Owen that this morning."

I throw a pillow at her. "Stop embarrassing him. And me."

"And it was quick of him to invite you to move in with him while you're here," Harper says. "You're both in a hurry and then pulling away. I'm getting whiplash."

I frown. "Me too."

Harper cocks her head. "Seriously, though. What is it about my brother that makes you want to rush into something serious? Don't you meet eligible men all the time?"

"He's different." I smile dreamily. "I just have all these wonderful memories from our summer together."

"Exactly," Harper says. "Memories. It's been nine years. If you're going to do this, you need to start over."

"Ooh, like they just met," Mackenzie says. "I can introduce you."

My brows scrunch at that bizarre idea. "That seems unnecessary—"

Olivia pokes her head in the doorway. She's wearing an old-fashioned floral nightgown. "If we're having a strategy session, I should be involved."

I smile. "Just talking about men and how confusing they are."

"Ah." She backs up. "I don't want to intrude on your personal life. It's important to keep the boundary between personal and professional."

"For God's sake, you live with your boss," Harper says. "Get in here."

Olivia walks in and gingerly takes a seat on the bed across from Harper.

"Olivia's right," I say. "I blurred the personal and professional with Owen, and I shouldn't have. Obviously, I have to fire him."

"I wouldn't advise that," Olivia says. "Why don't you just drop the personal until you can drop the professional? Don't mix the two. I say we hire the next bodyguard without consulting him. I suspect no one will meet his standards. He's unnecessarily complicating things."

"Because he wants her, but he can't admit how much," Harper says. "Wounded-bear alert."

Mackenzie stifles a laugh.

"That seems the most likely explanation," Olivia says.

My cheeks warm, pleased by the thought but also frustrated. "How can I *not* get personal with him? We were already very personal last night."

"I thought he was mad at you," Mackenzie says.

I lift one shoulder up and down. "We have incredible chemistry. It wouldn't take much to get him into bed again. That much I'm sure of."

Harper sticks her finger down her throat. "Besides the *eww* factor of that's my brother, please tell me you can control your hormones. You've been with the great Mick Schaeffer."

"There's no comparison," I say.

Mackenzie lifts a finger. "This is the real problem. You have Owen on a pedestal, looking at him through the foggy lens of the past. You don't know him now."

"He's improved in bed," I say.

"Again, *eww*," Harper says.

"And he's a protective, loving brother and son. You like working with him, right, Mackenzie?"

"Yes, but do you know what he likes to do in his free time?"

"He cruises for women with Nathan," Harper says with a sour note. "Nathan thinks he's God's gift to women. Such an ass."

"I hate arrogant men," Olivia says.

Harper leans over to give her a fist bump.

"Actually, Owen says Nathan's nobody's wingman on account of his supernaturally good looks," Mackenzie says.

"He did not say that," Harper says.

Mackenzie nods. "In so many words. You have to admit, Nathan is beautiful. I've never met a man in real life as perfectly made as he is."

"Then why don't you go for him?" Harper snaps.

Mackenzie smiles serenely. "He's my business partner, and I never mix business with pleasure. That's one rule of Mom's that makes total sense, especially when you own your own business with partners."

Olivia takes all of us in with a pointing finger. "Does anyone have a picture of Nathan? I could probably get him work."

Mackenzie pulls up his picture on her phone and shows her.

"Oh, yes," Olivia says.

Mackenzie looks at the picture with a smile and sets her phone down. "Olivia, why don't you come to our office party on Saturday at Happy Endings? You could meet Nathan. It wouldn't hurt our company to get some publicity. Nathan used to model in his teens and in college. People would want to meet with him, and then he'd wow them with his expertise."

Olivia nods once. "I'll be there. I was thinking beyond modeling, though. With an on-set acting coach, he could be a movie star."

I wave broadly. "Uh, ladies, can we please get back to my Owen issue?"

Olivia gives me a bland look. "We settled that. You're friends until we can find a replacement bodyguard. Then, if you choose, you can rekindle whatever you had, but with a fresh start." She claps once. "Very productive talk, ladies. Goodnight."

And then my assistant, who will one day rule the world, walks out.

～

After everyone's in bed, I can't resist sneaking downstairs to see Owen. We need to clear the air.

I find him stretched out on the couch with a blanket and pillow, reading something on his phone.

"That couch pulls out to a bed," I say.

He groans and sits up. "Please tell me you're not here for another relationship talk."

I blink a few times, stung. *Forget trying to patch things up between us!* "Actually, I just wanted to say you're fired."

"What!"

"As of Friday when I get your replacement in here."

"Oh."

I press my lips tightly together, willing the tears back as I finally let go of my hopes for us. "Also, you're fired as the love of my life."

"The *what*?"

I barrel on, embarrassed by my expectations. "I built up a lot in my mind about you based on the past. So from here on out, it will be strictly professional between us. After Friday, we don't need to see each other anymore."

He punches his pillow, rearranging it behind him. "Fine by me. I don't appreciate the way you roped me into your life. And my sister and cousin too."

"Fine," I say through my teeth.

"And, Shay, no more middle-of-the-night visits. It'll just give you the wrong idea."

I sputter, "I—you…good night!"

I march upstairs. So arrogant. *Wrong idea.* I won't have any more ideas where he's concerned. I'm seeing clearly now.

12

———

Owen

It's really over. Shayla's new bodyguard, Zander, started Friday morning, and I gotta say the guy seems like a good fit. He's a blackbelt, as well as a Marine veteran, and previously worked for a major pop star. And there's no worry with him living with four women since he informed us that he's getting married next New Year's Eve and will require a week off for the honeymoon with his husband in St. Bart's.

Not that I worried about Shayla getting involved with her bodyguard. She's all about separating the professional and the personal now. That's what she's told me about a hundred times this week, like some damn shield between us. I get it. It's what I wanted all along. Seriously, how many times do I have to get hurt by her?

I pace the downstairs of my house—living room, kitchen, dining room. Fortunately, I had my colonial-style house renovated, so it's an open floor plan, leaving lots of room for pacing.

What's Shayla doing right now? Is Zander paying attention to the little things? People in the neighborhood, unusual cars. He doesn't know the people in town. How would he know if someone didn't belong? This is why an insider is helpful, someone who knows Clover Park.

Why did she have to move to my town? Was it to get to me, or does she just want me for my family?

I stop pacing and send a quick text to Zander to check in.

Zander: *All clear.*

Well, I guess that's good. No issues. But is she at home, or is she on the move?

I go to ask Zander and put my phone away. I don't need to know.

The next day, I ring the bell at the home currently occupied by my cousin and sister and other people I don't need to worry about anymore.

An eye peers through the peephole, and then Mackenzie opens the door.

"Zander should be answering the door," I say. "Where is he?"

"Can't help yourself, can you? I answered because you said you wanted to talk to me about the office party."

"Where are they?"

"Relax. They stopped by Happy Endings so he could scope it out before the party tonight."

"Who's watching Shayla while Zander's scoping out the place?"

"Dad's there."

I relax marginally only because Uncle Josh is trained in hand-to-hand combat and has kept up his skills with krav maga. We talked about krav maga when I started studying it.

"What about the party did you want to talk about?" Mackenzie asks, stepping back for me to walk inside.

I step into the front room. "Who RSVP'd yes?"

"All the important people. I'm getting iced green tea. Want some?"

"No, thanks."

She heads to the kitchen.

I look at the sofa bed where I previously stayed. There's a

green blanket folded in a neat square and a pillow there. It's strange to think how easily I was replaced.

I join Mackenzie in the kitchen. "I don't think Shayla ever really needed me professionally at all."

Mackenzie leans back against the counter. "I think she did. She needed to feel safe, and that's exactly how you made her feel. And it sure didn't hurt our bottom line to be on her payroll for three weeks."

I grunt. "Who else will be there tonight?"

"I invited all our clients. A lot were away for the Memorial Day weekend, but I think we'll have a nice turnout. Low key, about a dozen clients, mostly single. Dad's bar has a great rep as a place to hang. Shay and Harper will be there too."

"Uh-huh."

"Owen?"

"Yeah?"

"If you could stop hating on her long enough, you'd see she's still in love with you."

"No, she's not. She's in love with my family. What we had is dead." I turn on my heel and head toward the door.

"Just keep your heart open!" She gasps. "Oh my God, I sound like my mother."

I'm only here because this party is for my company. Not to check on Shayla. Still, I can't help but notice she's surrounded by admirers in the back room of Happy Endings. I clench my teeth, my gut burning. Our clients, mostly men, fall all over themselves, flirting with her and taking selfies. Zander is standing just behind her, ready to step in. Problem is, he shouldn't let her be surrounded.

I'm moving across the room before I even realize it, fueled by adrenaline. Shayla's in danger. I work my way to the center of the group and take her by the hand. "Excuse me. I need a minute with Shayla."

"Owen!" She glances around. "Sorry."

I guide her over to a quiet corner of the room, Zander following at a distance.

I gesture him closer and speak in a low voice. "She should never be surrounded on all sides. You need to practice crowd control. Block access, or pull her from the situation."

He looks to Shayla for confirmation.

"He's probably right," she says. "I'll work on staying closer to you so I can't be surrounded."

"Got it," Zander says.

She turns to me. "I thought I fired you."

"You probably should have two bodyguards anyway. He can't be with you all the time like I was. Ask Olivia about getting another one."

"This is no longer your business. Now, if you'll excuse me." She heads over to Mackenzie and Harper.

I stand there for a stunned moment before heading to the buffet. How is her safety not my business? Of course it is. She made it that way the moment she asked me for help. Nothing can happen to her. She's too important. To everyone, not just me. She's Shayla freaking Adler, movie star.

I grab a small plate and help myself to a variety of hot appetizers, watching to be sure Zander's doing his job. He sticks close by Shayla while also scanning the room. I guess he's okay for the moment.

Mackenzie did a good job organizing the party. Nathan joins the group of women, and Harper abruptly walks away.

She spots me and walks over. "How's Zander working out?"

"He's okay, not great. Trainable."

Mackenzie goes over to the vintage jukebox and plays a slow song. Our client Raj asks her to dance and guides her on to the dance floor.

Harper adds some vegetables to a small plate and joins me. "Mixing business and personal," she says, watching Mackenzie and Raj. "We talked about this."

"It's just a dance," I say.

But then Nathan asks Shayla to dance, who looks

delighted. My shoulders tense. He holds her too close, talking the whole time. I bet he's piling on the compliments because she can't stop smiling. They met before when Shayla stayed with us that summer. Maybe she wishes she'd been with him that summer.

"She's too nice for him," Harper says.

"Who?"

"Who do you think? The couple you can't stop glaring at, Nathan and Shayla."

I grimace. "They're not a couple, and she's not that nice."

"Yes, she is. Really sincere."

I exhale sharply. "She's trying to manipulate my life to fit hers."

"To get a second chance with you."

"There's a reason it didn't work out the first time."

"The only way to move forward is to let go of the past."

"Where did you get that, a fortune cookie?"

"Fine. Stay miserable."

I rub the back of my neck. I am miserable without Shayla, but I can't see a way forward that works for both of us. I wish I could let go of the past because every time I think about the fact that she said she'd always love me and then kept in touch with my family and not me, I get angry all over again. I let out a breath. I'm tired of being angry about that.

Harper huffs. "Nathan is the most insincere man. Look at him just pouring on the flattery. You can't trust him. I should warn Shayla."

"What're you talking about? He's the most loyal guy I know. Why do you think I went into business with him?"

"Because he's rich."

"And he's loyal. He's my oldest friend. And he was yours too. What happened between you two?"

"Nothing. Absolutely nothing."

"Maybe you're the one who needs to let go of the past."

She sends me a dark look and chomps ferociously on a celery stalk.

The song ends, and another slow song starts. Mackenzie walks over to get some food and joins us.

"Raj asked me out," she says. "I know he's a client, but he seems really nice. And smart. He was telling me about a light saber he's creating that sounds like the real thing."

"What happened to that guy from the graduation-anniversary party?" Harper asks. "The waiter with the tribal tattoo."

"We hooked up," Mackenzie says matter-of-factly. "He's not with the sous chef, obviously, or I wouldn't have gotten involved. Anyway, I told him I didn't see it going anywhere, and he was relieved. What a jerk, right? At least he could've acted like he was hoping for more."

"You're a very complicated woman," Harper says.

Nathan comes up behind Harper. "Takes one to know one."

Harper whirls. "Done kissing up to Shayla? You know she has millions of fans to do that for her."

He holds out his hand to her. "Want to dance? I can kiss up to you too. Maybe then you'd stop giving me the glare of death every time our paths cross."

"No, thanks. I don't dance."

I spot Shayla surrounded by admirers again. Didn't we talk about this? She should never be surrounded.

I march over, leaving Harper and Nathan to their usual back-and-forth. He approaches; she advances in snarling defense. I wouldn't be surprised if she growled at him one day.

I take Shayla's hand. "Here you are, surrounded again. Dance with me."

She looks around. "Am I?" She steps out of the circle and on to the dance floor with me.

My pulse thrums through my veins as I pull her into my arms. She fits perfectly.

She rests her hands lightly on my shoulders. "I thought you were mad at me for…I'm not sure what."

"I'm not mad at you." I hesitate before admitting, "I miss you."

"Can we start over?" she asks with a smile that lights up her face. "I'm Shayla."

"Too late. I've seen you naked. The memory is burned into my brain."

She swats my arm. "Owen! Not so loud."

"Fine. We just met, and we're feeling each other out."

"Checking the vibe."

I laugh. "Sure."

We dance in silence for a few moments, the heat growing between us. Our chemistry is undeniable. That has to count for something. All I know is I'm not done with her.

The song ends, and we break apart. I miss the feel of her sweet curves against me.

"Dinner tonight. My place," I say.

She gives me a tentative smile. "Really?"

"Yes, really. Since we just met, I'm asking you out on our first date."

She smiles winningly. "I didn't catch your name."

"Lover."

She beams. "Nice to meet you, Lover. Should I bring Zander?"

I pull her close. "You don't need him when you've got me. Give him the night off. Actually, tell him he gets nights and weekends off. I'll pick up the slack. I'm sure he'd like to be with his partner."

"Owen, I'm not sure if that's a good idea. Mixing the personal and professional, I mean. Besides, Zander's okay with getting paid overtime for nights and weekends temporarily. They're saving for a house. I guess it makes sense to have a second guard in the future to give him breaks."

"I just want you all to myself." My voice sounds hoarse. I'm not used to admitting so much feeling stuff.

She loops her arms around my neck. "So you want to spend every night and weekend with me?"

"I want the option."

"That sounds like a commitment. What happened to Mr.

Casual?"

"He was always a front," I admit. "I don't know how to be casual with you."

She kisses me all over my face. I laugh, pure joy rushing through me. She's crazy about me. Always has been.

"I knew you were in there somewhere beneath all that grumpy defense!" she exclaims. "Let's get out of here. I'll go tell Zander the plan."

I wait while she talks to him. She turns to me, smiling with love in her eyes. My heart creaks open for the first time in years.

We rush out the back door, eager to be alone together.

I carry her upstairs to my bedroom, raw lust coursing through me.

She rubs my chest. "Did anyone ever tell you you're kinda romantic?"

"No."

"Well, you are. Carrying me to your bedroom is romantic."

I kick open the door to my room and set her down on the mattress. "It's faster this way."

She pouts. "Why not just toss me over your shoulder like a caveman next time?"

I strip out of my clothes. "Great idea." I pounce on her, and she squeals. God, I love this woman. I go stock-still. No, I don't love her. That's ridiculous. I can't possibly, not after…I swore I would never…I mean, yes, I have feelings. Deep feelings that never went away.

I just don't want to get burned again.

Her hand goes to my cheek. "What's wrong? You checked out on me."

I slowly shake my head. "Nothing."

"Then kiss me."

I do, her luscious lips drawing me in for more, her taste,

her scent. Next thing I know, I've stripped her bare, urgent need driving me, my hands all over her as I kiss her deeply.

She pushes at my shoulder, and I lift my head in question. She nudges me to my back and then straddles me. My body aches with need as she rains kisses from my lips to my chest and lower still.

I throw my arms back. She takes me in her mouth with the perfect amount of suction. Within moments, I'm teetering near the edge. I push her off.

She pushes her hair back and licks her lips. "I wasn't done."

I roll her to her back and grab a condom. "That felt too good."

She opens her legs to me, and my lust surges. "There's no such thing as too good."

I roll on the condom, get into position, and thrust home with a low groan of relief. She wraps her legs high around my waist, taking me deeper. God, it feels too good. Everything with her does.

I twine my fingers with hers on the mattress and kiss her, moving slow and steady. She grabs my ass and pulls me closer, urging me on. I thrust over and over, breathing hard. Our eyes meet and lock in a deep primal gaze that wraps around my heart.

My heart thunders in my chest. She loves me. I see it in her eyes, feel it pulsing between us like a living, breathing thing. I don't have to say anything. Neither does she. We both know.

And when we finish in a gasp of mutual pleasure, there's no question that we belong together.

"I love you." She runs her fingers through my hair, smiling. "I always have, Owen. I always will."

I tense, remembering when she said this the last time just before she walked out of my life. I try to convince myself this isn't the same, but something in me shuts down. Just as she starts to lose her smile, I kiss her, distracting her from the fact that I can't go there. This has to be enough.

13

Shayla

I never once took for granted that Owen would give me a second chance, but now that he has, all I can think is what took him so long? This weekend has been phenomenal. Granted, we spent most of it in bed, but now we're on our way to his parents' house for a big family barbeque by the pool for Memorial Day. I've never been happier.

He looks at me from the driver's side of his Mustang. "Shayla Adler, you're glowing."

I laugh. "It's all those sexy times." *And I love you.* I keep that to myself, very aware that he didn't return the *I love you* when I said it last time. I'm trying not to let it bother me. "So who's going to be here today?"

"Everyone."

"Same people as the anniversary-graduation party?"

"Yes, and my grandparents are flying in from North Carolina too."

"Oh, that's nice. How're they doing?"

"Great. Still active, enjoying retirement. Only person who couldn't make it is my uncle Rich. That's Mom's brother. He's busy with a soccer tournament for his son in Chicago."

"I just love your family."

He glances over at me with a smile. "Sometimes I think you only want me for them."

"Your family is just a bonus."

"I'm still not sure why I'm here," Olivia pipes up from the backseat.

I nearly forgot she was there. I've been so focused on Owen, and she's been busy on her phone.

"You're here because the party will be fun," I say. "You work too much, and it's not like you know anyone in town."

"And Mom is someone good to know in the industry," Owen says. "When you're running your own studio, her production company should be at the top of your list for women-forward movies and TV shows. It's all who you know, right?"

"Yes. That's why I'm really here," Olivia says, like Owen just reminded her. "Shayla, you know I don't enjoy nonproductive time. Nothing will derail me from my goals, not vacation time, not men, and definitely not parties. This job is a stepping stone. No offense. I'm here for you one hundred percent while we work together."

I fight a smile. How can someone so young sound so old?

"Understood," I say. "You'll like Claire. Don't go straight to shop talk. She's a really interesting person. Did you know she belongs to a romance book club, the Happy Endings Book Club? She even bought the rights to a few romance novels to make into movies. Like the Fierce trilogy and the movie I'm currently working on."

"Oh, now, that's interesting," Olivia says. "Scoping out intellectual property in a ready-made focus group. How do I get into this club?"

"Just ask and you're in," Owen says.

I perk up at that. "Really? Then I'll ask to join too. I've been wanting to read more." I turn toward Olivia. "Have you ever read a romance?"

"I read voraciously. Of course, I'm always thinking about how it might play as a movie."

"But do you read romance?"

"Yes," she admits, blushing.

My eyes widen. I've never seen no-nonsense Olivia blush. "Well, you'll have to tell me which authors to try."

"I could tell you," Owen says.

My head swivels toward him in surprise. "You read romance too?"

"Absolutely. Mom's got a full library of books. Every man should give romance a try. Sure didn't hurt me to better understand women, and I mean that in the dirtiest way possible." He gives me a smoldering look.

Now I'm blushing. Owen read his mom's romance novels and tried that stuff on me?

"Smart man," Olivia says.

"Thank you," Owen says smugly.

Now that Olivia and I are officially in the Happy Endings Book Club, we've joined Claire and friends in lounge chairs by the pool. We're following an intense discussion of their latest read, *Fiery Embrace*. Olivia takes notes on her phone.

"All I'm saying is, if they're going to start with a bang, it's disappointing not to see hot sex on the page at the end too," Madison says, leaning forward in her V-neck T-shirt to reveal a small hawk tattoo on her chest right over her heart. I want to ask her about it, but worry it's too personal.

Claire's here with her sisters-in-law Madison, Hailey, and a few other women who seem to be either sisters-in-law or honorary sisters-in-law married to Jake's honorary brothers. Claire introduced everyone as sisters.

Hailey pushes her white-framed sunglasses to perch on top of her strawberry-blonde hair. "We don't need to see sex on the page to know it happened. It was implied when they held hands on the way to her place. I thought this was an interesting take on romance, starting with a hookup and ending with holding hands. Like a romance in reverse."

Madison makes a face. "I don't read romance for hand-holding."

I can't stop staring at her tattoo every time she moves. It seems significant to place it over her heart.

"I see you're admiring my tat," Madison says to me.

"Did she just say tit?" Hailey whispers. "I swear, Mad—"

I laugh. "No, she said tat. I was curious about it. Does it mean something special? I noticed it's right over your heart."

She points over at her husband, Parker, helping Jake out at the barbecue. "Park got a hawk tattoo over his heart when he enlisted in the Air Force at eighteen. I was fifteen, madly in love with his oblivious self."

The women murmur amongst themselves.

"Remember when I gave you a makeover at Claire's wedding to open Park's eyes to the woman you'd become?" Hailey asks.

"You mean the beauty torture session?" Madison asks. "Hard to forget. And thanks, bitch."

Hailey beams.

Madison continues, "I never got over him, even after him being away for years, so I got a matching tattoo because he swooped in and stole my heart just like a hawk."

I place a hand over my heart. "Aww, so sweet."

"Just a fact," Madison says. "For him, the tat means think first and then take action, swooping in like a hawk." She shrugs. "It worked out." Her gaze meets Parker's, and he smiles at her.

"Sounds a little like you and Owen, Shay," Claire says from her chaise longue. "In love as teens and then reuniting later in life. Except Owen certainly wasn't oblivious. He was crazy about you, still is."

I can't help my smile. Everything's been going so well. Of course it's only been two days since he decided he wasn't mad at me anymore. I'd like to say he returns my love, but I'm not sure. It could just be sex for him. Though sometimes, there's a certain look in his eyes…

"Our relationship started with a fake engagement," a woman with shoulder-length dirty blond hair says. Sabrina Campbell, that's right. "Now Logan and I are happily married with three kids, two dogs, and a hamster." She wiggles her fingers at Logan, who's walking toward us with Josh, carrying wine bottles and glasses. He smiles warmly at her.

Logan and Josh stop to present their offerings to us.

The women exclaim over their thoughtfulness.

Josh leans down to kiss Hailey. Logan pours Sabrina a glass of wine and hands it to her.

"Thank you so much," Sabrina says to Logan. "Can you check on Deidre? She hasn't come out of the house yet. She's still upset she failed her driver's test. I think she'd feel better out here with her cousins. I tried, but she's so touchy with me lately."

"Leave it to me," Logan says confidently.

After Logan leaves, Sabrina shares their story—they had a fake engagement that she announced on TV, basically throwing him under the bus. He rose to the occasion.

That starts a domino effect with all the ladies sharing their love stories.

I like Charlotte's story. She finally agreed to a date with Ty after considering him to be too much of a player, and he wowed her with a dinner cruise on a borrowed boat that got stuck in the mud. They were basically trapped together on a boat for so long that they actually had to get to know each other.

But the best craziest story was Claire and Jake, which I'd never heard before. She was supposed to go on a blind date with his identical twin, Josh, but the twins pulled a switcheroo. Jake took out Claire as Josh, and Josh took out Hailey as Jake. It took a while for the women to realize the switch had happened since it was the first time Claire and Hailey had met Jake. Hailey just assumed the twins were very similar. When Claire found out, she told Hailey, who was so furious it launched an all-out war between Josh and Hailey until their parents fell in love and Josh and Hailey made up for the sake of the family.

"And because he was madly in love with me," Hailey says. She turns toward the pool and yells, "Right, Josh?"

He props his arms up on the side of the pool, water running in rivulets down his muscled chest and arms. "Right."

"He can't even hear me," Hailey tells us. "He just agrees."

Claire points at Hailey. "Now that's the sign of a man who knows the secret to a happy marriage."

We all laugh, even Olivia, who finally stopped taking notes long enough to really listen to the women's stories.

I shriek as I'm suddenly airborne. Owen just scooped me up in a sneak attack. Mmm…I'm cradled in his arms against his bare warm chest. This reminds me of how he romantically carried me to bed.

Wait, where's he taking me? I look back to the women, who wave bye.

"You won't get any help from them," he says.

We're almost at the pool.

"Owen! I'm wearing my coverup. Don't you dare dump me in the water."

"I would never…" He walks to the deep end. "Take a deep breath."

I give in to the inevitable and comply, but he doesn't drop me. He jumps into the deep end with me!

We surface near each other. I push my hair back and splash him in the face. He ignores the splashes, steadily advancing on me until he finally grabs me and kisses me. A rush of heat goes through me in the cool water.

"Payback, Campbell," I say in my most menacing voice before swimming to the side.

He follows me. When we get to the side, he wraps an arm around my waist and pulls me close. I put a hand on his chest and push, but he doesn't budge. "You soaked my coverup."

He dips his head, bringing us kissing close. My pulse accelerates. "Maybe I don't like you covered up."

His lips meet mine with a soft brush and then another before finally settling on mine in a tender kiss that undoes me. This man. This wonderful man.

A splash of water hits the side of my face. We break apart to find his cousins splashing us.

"Who's up for a chicken fight?" Finn asks.

Owen turns to me in question.

"Hell yeah, we'll kick your ass," I say.

Owen laughs.

"Where's Olivia?" Finn asks. "I want her on my team."

"Olivia!" I wave to her, where she's reading a book next to Claire and friends. "Come in! We're playing chicken."

She shakes her head. "I'm not wearing a bathing suit." She told me before she doesn't own one because she hates the way she's crammed into the tight material and would never dare wear a bikini. Instead she's wearing a loose navy sundress that ends at the knees. At least she traded her steel-toed boots for flip-flops.

"What you have on is fine," Finn says. "Come on. You're on my team."

Olivia's hand goes to her throat. "Me?"

"Yes," he says with a laugh.

"No, thanks."

"Why not?"

"I'm reading."

"You can read anytime. Come on, it'll be fun."

"Yeah, come on, Olivia," I call. "What are you, chicken?"

Finn gestures for me to settle down. "Who brought you your favorite double espresso on Saturday *and* Sunday morning? You owe me one."

Ooh, this is new info. He was probably painting at the house and brought it then.

Olivia pushes her sunglasses to the top of her head. "And I appreciate that, but I'm too heavy for you."

"Try me." His voice sounds husky and inviting.

Claire and friends get quiet. Now all eyes are on nineteen-year-old Finn. Mackenzie's little brother sounds all man and flirty as hell with an older woman. Not that Olivia is old at twenty-three. It's just a big difference compared to nineteen.

"I'm not good at games," Olivia says lamely.

While Finn tries to coax her in with an interesting sequence of hand gestures—you, me, pound chest, champions—Nathan rises out of the water with Mackenzie on his shoulders. Harper gets Cooper to lift her up.

Owen bends in the water for me, and I climb on. We rise up together.

"We need four pairs to make it even," Finn says to Olivia.

"I'll do it," Madison says, rising from her lounge chair.

Finn makes his way to the side of the pool. "Thanks, Aunt Mad, but I really want Olivia."

He gets out of the pool and walks over to Olivia. Water drips off his trim muscular body. Her jaw drops as she looks up at him from her lounge chair. Damn, I can't hear the conversation from here.

A few moments later, he sits next to her and grabs a towel to dry off. She looks mystified by his presence.

"Play without me!" Finn yells over to us.

"Park!" Madison calls. "I need you for chicken."

He glances at us in position in the pool. "Are they ready for the fiercest competitor in the world?"

Harper rubs her hands together. "I can take her this year."

Parker pulls off his shirt and jumps in the pool. Madison joins him a moment later, stopping to give him a hard kiss before climbing on his shoulders.

Owen rushes toward Nathan, and I battle Mackenzie on his shoulders, who's stronger than she looks. Geez, talk about fierce. Good thing I work out daily.

Owen retreats and rushes forward at an angle, giving me just the advantage I need. Mackenzie goes down, and Nathan tips sideways too.

I look over just as Harper and Cooper get toppled by Madison. Parker turns her toward us.

"Oh shit," I say.

Madison laughs like a loon. Her twenty-something sons—

Mason, Michael, Maddox, and Miles—gather by the side of the pool, cheering her on and taking bets. What must their house have been like growing up with a tough mom like Madison? They probably had gladiator fights in the backyard.

Owen rushes forward, and Madison grabs my arms, so I grab hers. We grapple for a few moments before Owen retreats.

I'm sure I have Madison-sized finger marks on my arms, but there's no time to check because Parker and Owen rush forward again.

This time she goes for my shoulder, trying to knock me off balance.

"Hang on, Shayla!" one of Madison's sons yells. "My money's on you."

Oh, that's nice.

Splash! I'm down.

I pop up to hear Madison yelling at one of her identical twins. "That'll teach you to bet against me. Ha!"

"Someone had to take the opposite side," he says. "What's the point of betting otherwise?"

She inclines her head. "Good point. Still I'm glad you lost." She raises her arms in a V of victory. Her sons cheer for her.

A moment later, Parker ducks under water, slipping her off his shoulders.

"Let's do it again!" Madison gestures to Claire and friends. "Ladies, get in here!"

"It's barbaric," Hailey says. "No, thank you."

"Your daughter played," Madison says.

Hailey smiles serenely. "And I'm very proud of Mackenzie for forging her own path. Where is my sweet warrior queen?"

Mackenzie comes out of the house with a towel wrapped around her waist, carrying a pitcher of what looks like sangria. Harper's carrying a platter with vegetables.

Nathan's gaze tracks the sway of Harper's hips in her skirt coverup as she walks by. It's really too bad she hates him.

~

I sigh. I wish every day could be like this. After hours of fun splashing in the pool and a delicious barbecue, I'm sitting on a lounge chair between Owen's legs, his arms wrapped around me. We're gathered around a firepit, making s'mores with the younger group while Claire's crowd is inside in the kitchen and the man cave in the basement. Olivia went with the older crowd. Sometimes I worry she's missing out on her twenties. All she thinks about is the future and what she wants to achieve.

"What's the craziest thing you've ever done?" Nathan asks, pointing his beer bottle at Owen.

"Quit my job and go into business with you," Owen returns.

One corner of Nathan's mouth tilts up, and he points the bottle at me next.

"In between acting jobs, I worked as a fluffer," I say with a straight face.

Owen leans down to look at me and must read the truth in my eyes because he relaxes.

"Get out," Nathan says. "For real?"

"What's a fluffer?" Finn asks.

"It's the woman who keeps porno actors fully aroused between takes," Nathan says to Finn.

"Whoa," Finn says.

"Liar," Harper says.

I laugh. "Well, I had to make it interesting. I've never done anything crazy."

"Next!" Nathan says, pointing the bottle at Harper.

"Pass," she says.

"You can't pass," he says.

"Yes, I can." She takes a bite of s'more, pointing to her full mouth.

"Fine, Mackenzie?" he asks.

She tosses her hair back over one shoulder. "I once had a

fling with a guy who wore a Darth Vader costume in bed. We met at a comic con."

"My mom has a Darth Vader costume," Mason says. "Sure you didn't hook up with your aunt Madison?"

"Eww!" Mackenzie exclaims. "Yes, I'm sure. He took off the helmet before—this conversation is entirely too sexual to have in front of my cousins and brothers. Next topic, please!"

Harper jerks her thumb toward Nathan. "He started it, the perv."

"Takes one to know one," Nathan returns. "Besides, I said what was the craziest thing you've done, not what was the sexual thing. Shayla got us started down that path."

"Please forgive me for being interesting," I say.

"Are we out of wine?" Mackenzie asks.

Owen pulls another bottle from the ice bucket next to our chair.

"Thank you." Mackenzie unscrews the cap and pours a generous portion for herself. She offers the bottle. "Anyone else?"

Harper reaches for it, pours herself a refill, and passes it back to me. I put it back in the ice bucket.

"You know what sucks about your twenties?" Mackenzie asks.

"All that freedom?" Finn asks sarcastically.

"Oh, please, Mom and Dad give you plenty of freedom," Mackenzie says. "More than I had. That's what happens when you're the oldest. By the time they got to you, they were worn out."

Finn shakes his head. "I can't wait to get my own place. College gave me a taste of real independence. Now I'm back to chores and not bringing women home."

"Olivia's right inside," his older brother, Cooper, says teasingly. "Go for it. If you're lucky, she'll take you back to her place."

Mackenzie waves that away. "Olivia lives with me, so forget it, little bro. Anyway, what sucks about your twenties is all the fucking weddings. I've spent a fortune in bridesmaid dresses I'll never wear again as my college friends get married one by one. I just got another invitation in the mail. It's torture. I swear, love is just big business."

"Don't let your mom hear you say that," I say.

Mackenzie rolls her eyes. "I can hate weddings while still respecting what she's achieved. I've got three weddings to go to in June, one of them all the way up in Vermont. That's basically my entire June. And I'll be wearing a hideous dress to make the bride look good, eating overcooked fish, and doing yet another round of funky chicken. Funky chicken isn't fun and will never be fun. Who invented that?" She finishes on a high note of indignation.

Everyone stares at her.

She collects herself and says in a much calmer tone, "Of course I'm happy for my friends."

More like jealous. I keep that to myself.

"Yeah," Nathan says. "I've been to my share of weddings too. If I ever get married, it'll be a courthouse ceremony, and then we'll do it up with an awesome honeymoon."

Mackenzie goes on as if he hasn't spoken. "And the worst part is, I never have a plus one, so I get stuck dancing with my assigned groomsman, and then the rest of the night just sit there and watch all the happy couples dance. Not that I want a wedding date. I'm just saying I don't enjoy the whole ritual of forced coupledom. Not fun."

"Maybe you should go clubbing to counteract all that couple stuff," Owen says.

"God, I haven't been to a club in so long." Mackenzie looks around the circle. "Who's in for next weekend?"

"I'll go," Harper says.

"I'm up for it," Nathan says.

Harper shoots him a dark look before turning to me. "How about you, Shayla?"

"It sounds fun, but it's not the safest place for me."

"Oh, that's right. Sometimes I forget you have a following. I wonder if Mom ever went to clubs. I should ask her."

Harper stands and goes inside, presumably to ask Claire.

Nathan watches her go before asking us, "Did you see the way she looked at me when I said I was up for clubbing? Like I'm death to good times."

Mackenzie goes to pat his shoulder and misses. "Aww, don't take it personally. She just doesn't like you."

"Why not? I'm very likeable. Ask anyone. Chicks dig me."

"Might have something to do with the fact you say chicks," Owen says.

"There's something seriously wrong with your sister," Nathan says to Owen.

"Harper's always had her own agenda, and the rest of us aren't in on it," Owen says.

"Well," I venture, "maybe she's jealous because she thinks you're into Mackenzie. You did play chicken with her earlier, and then when she suggested a club, you agreed."

"For God's sake, Mackenzie's like a sister to me." He puts a hand on top of her head. "Right?"

She puts her hand on top of his head. "Right, little bro."

I laugh.

"Hey, Shayla, sorry to interrupt." Frankie's voice sounds low near my ear.

I turn to him, still smiling. "What's up?"

"I found a car parked just outside the gate, using a camera with a telephoto lens. When I approached, they drove away. Male driver, alone."

I stop smiling, my heart accelerating. "It could've been someone trying to sell a picture of two famous people."

"Could've been," he says. "I just wanted you to be aware. I'm going to review the security tape for the license plate."

A chill runs through me.

My fears are confirmed a short time later. The license plate is the same as the car Matt was driving the last time he watched me.

"It doesn't matter where I go," I whisper to Owen. "I can never feel safe."

He pulls me into his arms. "You're safe with me."

But for how long?

14
———

I'm so pissed off. I don't want Matt anywhere near Shayla or Mom. We're in the kitchen now with Mom and her friends because Shayla didn't feel safe anymore. I hate that Matt ruined what was otherwise a great day. Shayla doesn't often get to enjoy herself like this, surrounded by people who love her.

Not that *I* love her. I refuse to let that happen. I know better than to open my heart to a woman who'll leave on a moment's notice for the next shiny project. I'll never come first with her. That's a deal breaker for me. If I did get serious with someone, I'd put them first and expect the same. I should probably tell her I don't see a future for us, but then she'll bail, and I'm not ready to say goodbye yet.

I know, I know. It's why I tried to resist her in the first place, but there's no putting the genie back in the bottle. Or the lust and like, deep like, and, oh, hell. I just can't help myself where she's concerned, even knowing the risk.

"I'm so sorry I put you in danger," Shayla says tearfully to Mom.

"Oh please," Mom says. "I'm in no more danger now than I ever was. Paps and stalkers come with the territory."

Shayla gives her a watery smile. Mom hugs her.

Mom smooths Shayla's hair back. "You did nothing wrong. You can't let the crazies make *you* crazy. You have to live your life."

"I know," Shayla says in a small voice. Matt really shook her up.

"And if it's not Matt, it'll be some other guy or a woman," Mom says. "You know when Missy Barnes had that hit movie, she attracted a woman who threw rotten fruit at Missy's boyfriend whenever they went out in public."

Shayla looks at me, horrified.

"That's not helping," I say.

Mom lifts her palms. "Ah, well, I'll let you step in here." She goes over to Dad, who wraps an arm around her.

I pull Shayla close and whisper in her ear, "Let's go back to my place."

"Okay."

We say our goodbyes and get in the car with Olivia.

Shayla's quiet on the drive home. I glance at the backseat, where Olivia stares out the window into the dark.

"Did you have a good time, Olivia?" I ask.

"What's the deal with your cousin Finn?"

"What do you mean?"

"Like, why does he keep talking to me and flirting and bringing me espresso?"

Our eyes meet in the rearview mirror. "I guess because he's into you."

"No, that can't be it. Is he trying to get into the industry? Does he have a thing for curvy women?"

"Uh, I don't think he's trying to use you to get into the industry. He could always ask Mom for help. Besides, he hasn't even picked a major yet." I'm not touching that curvy-woman remark.

"I just can't imagine I'm his type," Olivia says.

"Why wouldn't you be?" Shayla asks, speaking for the first time since we left the party. "You're pretty, smart, and competent."

Olivia ignores the compliment. "And he's too young for

me. I told him that, and he said age doesn't matter between consenting adults."

I fight back a laugh. Finn sounds wise beyond his years.

"We need to hire a new painter," Olivia says. "It's very awkward now with Finn. Owen, could you let him know he's not my type?"

"Sure, if it comes up," I say.

Shayla turns around in her seat. "Can you just be polite to Finn and let him keep painting our place? He needs the money to buy a car."

"Fine," Olivia says. "I'll find out his schedule and avoid him. I really don't have time for dating with my five-year plan." She takes her phone out and starts tapping away. Probably emailing Finn for his painting schedule.

I glance over at Shayla. "Did you have a good time before Frankie let us know the bad news?"

"I was having the *best* time, and I hate that something like this could take that away from me. Now I'm scared and pissed off at the same time. I don't know how your mom can be so relaxed about it."

"I'm sure she's learned to live with the cost of fame. Do you ever think of stepping out of the spotlight? Maybe doing something else?" I hold my breath, hope making my limbs feel lighter.

"God, no. I love acting, and I'm lucky I get as much work as I do. There's a time limit on that. One day you're hot, and the next you're nothing."

"She's right," Olivia says.

"Mom's had a long career," I say.

"That's the exception, especially for a woman," Shayla says. "I'd love to follow in her footsteps, but that's not in my control."

"Have you thought about directing?" I ask. "Mom often hires women directors and likes to film locally in Connecticut and New York." Obviously I'm hoping Shayla will stick around for a while. If I knew there was a way we could make it work for both of us, I could go all in.

"One day I could see myself directing," she says. "For now I'm enjoying acting. Do you like what you do?"

"Yeah, I do. I love being my own boss, setting my own hours. It's great to work with Nathan and Mackenzie. We complement each other. Well, I should say Mackenzie complements me and Nathan. It works."

"Have you talked to them about going with me to Vancouver? Mackenzie told me your company is looking for new markets, and I'd like to see you there." She puts a hand on my leg, and I tell myself not to get sucked in. I don't want to follow her from project to project. I'm my own man with a life here.

"And then what?" I ask.

"Then we'd go from there," she says. "See where it goes."

I'm quiet. Shayla keeps talking about a future with me, but it all depends on me following her around. Now I'm starting to wonder if it was a mistake to let things get this far.

Olivia pipes up, ever practical, "If you want, I could contact the studio and see what kind of numbers we're looking at for a security job. That might help your decision."

"Great idea," Shayla says. "Mackenzie said she'd like to visit me there. You could both go and check out the job. I'd really like you there in addition to Zander."

I stiffen. I thought she was asking so we could be together. Instead she wants me to fill out her security team.

"I've got a big potential job in DC," I say. "Mackenzie says it's looking good. We'll know for sure at the end of next week. If we get it, I'll be in DC for three months."

"Can't Nathan do it?" she asks.

"Nathan promised he'd spend a couple of weeks at Martha's Vineyard with his family, so he'd miss part of it. It's best if one person takes the lead and sticks with it. And before you ask, Mackenzie doesn't do the high-tech work. She's more operations and accounting. The engine that keeps our company going."

"Okay," she says quietly.

Long moments pass. I glance over at her sad expression.

Dammit. I can't take how sad she looks. I'm the one who makes her feel protected and safe.

"I'll think about it," I say.

"You will?" She sounds genuinely surprised.

"Yeah."

"Should I check in with the studio?" Olivia asks.

"Yes, go ahead," Shayla says, beaming at me.

My chest puffs out with pride. It's nice to be needed, even if it's just for security purposes. This doesn't mean I'm going to follow her from project to project. There's a real possibility this studio gig is bigger than the government contract. I owe it to the company to at least look into it.

Shayla

The week goes by in a blur between work and nights with Owen. The best part is things are looking promising for him to work on the Vancouver location. They've been having a problem with people stealing equipment and selling it on the black market. I hadn't realized that when I invited him. I just thought it would be great to make his job and my job fit together. I still have hope for our future, even if Owen pulls away at times. He's not all in yet, but when he sees how it could work, then he'll relax.

Tonight we're at a friend's Broadway show. It's a sold-out Saturday night showing. My friend Rodney is a triple threat —acts, sings, and dances. I can carry a tune, but I could never do what he does. And forget about dancing. I stick to slow dancing, and if there's no one with a camera, I'll bop around the dance floor a bit too.

We're sitting in the front row. I peek over at Owen to see if he's enjoying himself. Hard to tell. It's an upbeat musical, a reimagining of *Romeo and Juliet* with a happy ending. Rodney plays Romeo. He's heart-stopping gorgeous. Really. He was stopped on the street as a teen and signed to a lucrative modeling contract. Musicals are his true love.

The show ends to a standing ovation.

"Did you like it?" I ask Owen.

He nods. "Really good."

"Come on, we're invited backstage."

We slip out of our seats to a side door where a guard, along with Zander, guides us through the backstage area to Rodney's dressing room.

A few minutes later, he joins us. "Shayla! Thanks for coming. I haven't seen you in forever." He hugs me. We're nearly always on opposite coasts.

"I know, right? This is Owen Campbell."

Rodney shakes his hand. "Rodney Bell, nice to meet you. So what did you think? We're still working out the kinks in the show. It's only been a week, and the choreographer is still making changes."

"It was great," I say. "Really fun."

"It's always fun when the leads don't die in the end," Owen says.

Rodney laughs. "That's fair, though it would be fun to play out a tragic death scene. Are you coming to the after-party? They booked this awesome Korean barbecue place for us. We're celebrating making it through the first week."

I check in with Owen, who smiles. "We'll be there!"

After delicious appetizers of kimchi pancakes, chicken wings, and barbecue chickpeas at Rodney's table, Owen and I settle in the upstairs lounge. Jazz music plays on low volume, and people relax on cushy chairs, sofas, and even a few beanbags.

The actor who played Mercutio stops by. Sam Miller. We've met before.

"You look so familiar," he says to Owen.

"I get that a lot," Owen says. "You were great."

"Thanks. Were you in *The Fantasticks*?"

"No."

"Ensemble for *Rent*?"

"No."

"Oh, sorry. So rude. I'm Sam."

"Owen."

"And of course I know the magnificent Shayla. How do you know Owen?"

I lean my head against Owen's shoulder. "We had a summer romance when we were teens, and now we've reunited."

Owen grimaces. "It sounds like a teen movie."

"That's sweet," Sam says. "Well, enjoy yourselves."

After he leaves, I ask Owen, "Why didn't you tell him your mom is Claire Jordan? That's why you look familiar to him."

He looks to the ceiling. "Because then we'd have the whole Mom conversation, her movies, what she's really like, what it was like growing up with a famous mom. I'd rather not get into it."

"Oh. I'd be proud to talk about a mom like Claire."

"I'm proud of her. I just don't need to talk about her with every random person who recognizes me from one of her events."

A group of twenty-something women head over to us, their eyes glued to Owen.

One of them approaches him. "Rafael Jordan-Campbell?" Then when she gets up close, she says, "Sorry, wrong person. Rafael has these stunning blue eyes. Yours are nice, though."

Owen shoots me a look. Only Rafael uses his mom's maiden name along with his dad's name because he's a photographer, and the name helps open doors.

"Rafael is his brother," I say.

"Very cool," she says. "I'm Brooke. He took my picture for my latest headshot. I always hoped I'd run into him again. Can you give him my number?"

"Sure," Owen says.

She says her phone number slowly and clearly while he texts it to Rafael along with her name. She walks away with her friends, looking pleased.

"So Rafael's the more famous brother," I tease.

"He's usually behind the camera, but he enjoys mixing it up with all different kinds of people."

Eventually, we make our way over to a round corner booth that seats twelve people. The dance captain, Ben, holds court with one funny quip after another. Owen joins in, seeming more relaxed now. I sit back and sigh. This is good. Owen's comfortable hanging with creatives. Now that the timing's better, I can see him fitting into my life seamlessly.

∿

Owen

Around midnight, everyone heads home. The cast has to perform again tomorrow night, and no one wanted to stay out too late. Fine by me, I'm eager to get Shayla back in my bed. I feel like a horny teenager, always wanting her. It's hard to be close to her and not want to get naked. Our chemistry was intense from the start and has only grown now that we have the freedom to take our time in bed. My pulse races just thinking about what I want to do to her. Even knowing it can't work out, part of me doesn't care.

She cares.

I push down the guilt over not telling her I see Vancouver as a temporary reprieve. I'm tired of looking toward the dismal future where our relationship inevitably falls apart as we take our separate paths. I just want to enjoy the now.

I entwine my fingers with hers as we head to the front door of the restaurant. She smiles up at me, and my heart stutters. I look straight ahead, energy coursing through me at our electric connection.

I halt suddenly a few feet from the door. There's a mob of paparazzi waiting.

I turn to Zander. "Back door."

"Is this all for me?" Rodney exclaims dramatically, shooing Shayla behind him. He's awesome.

"For both of us," the woman who plays Juliet says. "Let's give them what they want."

They walk out the front door together, holding hands and smiling. We don't wait around to see if they get their own photo session.

Zander leads the way to a back door. He already scoped out the restaurant as soon as we arrived. He goes through first.

A flurry of movement has me tucking Shayla behind me.

"I'll sue!" a man yells as he runs down the street with Zander on his heels.

And this is why Shayla needs two bodyguards because if one takes off for some reason, there needs to still be someone with her.

Shayla turns to me. "That was a pap, right?"

"We'll find out in a minute. Zander's on his way back."

Zander jogs up to us. "He got into a waiting car, and I didn't want to leave you for too long. It was Matt, carrying a camera to blend with the paparazzi. He must've broken away from the group when he saw you turn away from the front door."

Shayla squeezes my hand tightly, her face pale.

Zander scowls. "He probably called the paparazzi in the first place in hopes of drawing Shayla to an alternate exit."

"Did he have a weapon?" I ask.

"Not that I saw. Just the camera and what he said was an urgent message for Shayla."

Shayla's hand goes to her throat. "What was the message?"

"It doesn't matter what the message was," I say. "There's nothing he has to say that should affect your life in any way."

"But what if it was a death threat?"

"More likely a declaration of love," I say just to reassure her. "The man is not well. Who knows what he'll say?"

"I never heard what it was," Zander says. "I told him I had an urgent message for him, and that was, he was about to get arrested for violating his restraining order. He took off after that."

Shayla takes a quivering breath.

"You okay?" I ask her.

"Mmm-hmm," she says. "Let's go."

As soon as we get into the car, she bursts into tears. I haul her into my lap, wrapping my arms around her.

"You're safe," I murmur near her ear. "Everything's okay."

She sniffles and rubs my chest. "Sometimes it gets to be too much. It always seems like when I finally get to relax and enjoy myself, there he is."

"Well, he's not going to visit you at work. Too much security."

"I need a second guard. I don't know what I would've done if you weren't there when Zander took off after him. What if there was another threat?"

"I was thinking the same thing."

She clings to me a little tighter.

Shayla

Despite my earlier scare, I'm relaxed by the time we get back to Owen's place. Probably helped that he held me for the whole drive. I don't think I've ever felt safer than when I'm in his arms.

Once we're in bed, I say, "You seemed like you fit right in at the after-party."

"Rubbing elbows with the glamorous crowd was part of my life for a long time."

I climb on top of him and hug him with all the love I'm feeling. I prop up on my elbows to look at him. "I can see a future for us. You'll fit right in."

His big hand wraps around the back of my neck and pulls me in for a kiss. He's tender, showing me his love, even if he can't say it. Desire unfurls within me, relaxing every muscle as he holds me close.

Long moments later, he rolls me under him. And then he takes his time, slowly stripping me out of my clothes, kissing and touching every inch of exposed skin. He's taking care with me, knowing how shaken I was earlier, and I love him for it. My body hums with desire, every nerve ending sparking as his lips graze over my skin. I reach for the button on his shirt, and he leans back on his heels, taking off his shirt himself.

I sit up and run my hands over his warm heated skin, loving the feel of his powerful chest and rippling abs. I'm bursting to tell him just how much I love him, but don't want to risk not hearing it back. Instead I pour it all into a long passionate kiss.

He breaks the kiss, his dark eyes smoldering as he steps out of bed to strip out of the rest of his clothes. "I want you so bad."

I open my arms to him. "You have me."

He joins me again, stroking my hair back from my face as he gazes into my eyes. His voice is gravelly. "Shayla."

My name sounds like a declaration of love. His lips meet mine, his tongue spearing inside as his hand runs down my body to pleasure central.

He shifts to my side, his fingers working magic while he kisses me long and deep. A haze of intense pleasure overwhelms me. My hips rock in time to his rhythm, bringing me up, up, up, higher and higher until I break with a cry and collapse to the mattress.

I hear the rustle of a condom wrapper, and then he's back, settling between my legs and sliding home. He frames my face with his hands, kissing me deeply as we're joined as closely as two people can be.

He lifts his head, gazing into my eyes as he slowly thrusts, every movement bringing us closer together. A connection of two souls lost without the other. My emotions soar along with the pleasure, filling me up, drawing me closer and closer to the man I love.

He nuzzles into my neck before thrusting harder and

faster, taking me on a wild ride that leaves us both panting. I go off, my insides clenching around him, and that sets him off. He buries himself deep with a long groan and collapses on top of me.

I hold him tight.

After a few moments, he whispers in my ear, "I'll go with you to Vancouver."

My heart pounds harder. "You will?"

He lifts his head and smiles. "I'll tell the DC people Nathan will do it, but it has to be a two-week-later start date."

I beam. "I'm so happy."

He rolls off me, lying on his back. "I just want you to be safe."

I prop up on an elbow to look at him. "That's the only reason?"

"And because it could be a good new market for us."

"What about us?"

He shifts to kiss me. "We'll have nights to ourselves, I hope."

I roll out of bed.

"Hey, where're you going?" he asks.

"I'm going to get ready for bed."

"You already did that."

"Well, I'm going to do other private things," I say, escaping to the bathroom.

I close the bathroom door and lean against it, scrunching my eyes shut tight, willing the tears away. Obviously Owen isn't in the same place as me. In fact, this trip sounds like a job for him. He wants to be my guard and keep me safe. Oh, and hook up every night. That's what I am to him. A good time.

I dash at a tear. Shit. I went about this all wrong. What I really wanted was for him to be with me no matter what. Now he's going to Vancouver for work, and that's all it is to him. My throat tightens. I got what I wanted but not what I needed. I let out a shaky breath. It's my own fault for not telling him just how much I love him. How much I want him in my life. I was afraid it would scare him off. It probably would have.

I just wanted things to be different than last time. I didn't want to be the one leaving for a job without him. I bend over, resting my hands on my knees, tempted to sink to the floor. I don't know how to fix this.

He knocks on the door.

I move away from it. "Come in."

He opens it. "Can we get back to the kissing part now?" It's an apology of sorts with that charming smile.

I lift my chin. "You can't go to Vancouver just for sex."

"It's work and sex."

At my dark look, he picks me up and throws me over his shoulder. "Owen!"

"Someone needs more good loving to get that grumpy look off their face," he says, slipping his hand between my legs.

I moan softly.

He lowers me to the bed and smiles down at me. "Now that's more like it."

"Am I really just a job and sex for you?"

"How can you even ask me that with our history?"

My lips part in surprise. Just as I realize he's neatly evaded the question, he spreads my thighs and lowers his head, and all thoughts fly from my mind.

15

———

Owen

"We didn't get the DC project," Mackenzie tells me first thing in our Monday afternoon meeting. It's just the two of us. Nathan's out on a job.

"I thought it was a sure thing. Did they say why?"

She grimaces. "They were pissed about the change in schedule with Nathan coming on two weeks later than anticipated."

Because I'm going to Vancouver.

"Seriously? It's only two weeks."

She lifts her palms. "They didn't feel the end date would work, and they had another company that was also at the top of their list, so they're going with them."

I scrub a hand over my face. This is my fault. And the Vancouver job isn't even a sure thing.

"I screwed up," I say.

"It's not your fault."

"Yes, it is. I let a major client slip away for the potential of a new job when, let's face it, my dick was doing the thinking."

She gives me a deadpan look. "Never trust a tiny brain."

∾

That night when Shayla shows up at my place, I tell her about losing the DC job over a late dinner of her favorite vegetable stir-fry. I'm always hungry after she cooks. She makes the effort, though, so I keep my mouth shut.

"I'm sorry to hear it," she says. "Honestly, it sounds like they would've been a tough client to work for the way they got upset over such a minor schedule change. You're probably better off."

"We needed the business."

She reaches across the table to hold my hand. "I get that, but don't worry, I'm sure the Vancouver job will make up for it. Olivia called over, and at the very least, they'd like you to secure equipment to stop the rash of robberies they're dealing with. They're open to more if you solve that problem first."

My shoulders relax. We're supposed to leave for Vancouver in a little over two weeks. "When did she talk to them?"

"Today. Olivia said you should give the producer a call early tomorrow before they start filming for the day. They're out there now finishing up a TV movie." She pulls her phone out and sends me the contact info.

"Thanks, Shayla. You really came through for me."

"Of course! You can count on me."

I want to believe her, but with our history, it's tough. I take her hand and kiss her palm.

She gazes into my eyes with such warmth my heart stutters. She still loves me. It's right there in her eyes. I need to take a risk.

"I didn't just invite you to Vancouver for the job, you know," she says.

"I know." Part of me always knew, I just didn't want to risk getting in too deep.

"I don't want things to end the way they did last time with my job coming between us." Her voice chokes. She takes a deep breath. "I want a future that's a win-win for both of us. That's why I thought getting you work alongside mine was ideal. Truth is, I'd be happy if you wanted to be with me as much as I want to be with you."

My heart does a funny flip-flop. Her sincerity reaches out and wraps around me like a warm hug. I pull her out of her seat and into my lap, kissing her. If we're still this happy in Vancouver, maybe we do have a future.

Shayla

It's Friday night, and I can't wait to get back to Clover Park. I'm stretched out across the long backseat of the car. My bodyguard, Zander, is in the front passenger seat with the driver. Olivia came back earlier to take care of a few errands.

Work was hard on my body physically this week with all the fight scenes. I'm looking forward to sleeping in over the weekend and seeing Owen and my friends again.

Olivia showed me pictures of my house's interior, and it's really starting to look good with the fresh paint and decorative touches Mackenzie added. One day I'd like to live there again. It's a good house for a family.

I close my eyes, and images of Owen flash through my mind:

His warm brown eyes gazing into mine while we make love.

Sprawled naked on his stomach in bed, grumbling, "Bye," as I leave at five a.m.

His smile when I return home that lights up his face.

I've got it bad. If things go well in Vancouver, I'm thinking of proposing to him. He proposed to me before, and now it's my turn. I can do the unconventional and make my own path in life.

My phone rings, and I check the screen. It's my agent, Will. He's a bulldog, always fighting to get me more money and better opportunities. He likes to say, "Where there's a Will, there's a way."

I answer. "Hey, Will. How's it going?"

"Great! You remember the untitled Oliver Nuckowski project that was working its way through the studios?"

I sit up. "Of course I remember." Oliver is a writer/director known for epic stories with big budgets that kill at the box office. I read the script for his latest project set in a fantasy world with a quest led by a kickass woman, Nala. She's everything—smart, fearless, funny, but also capable of deep love. The script made me laugh and cry. I met with him months ago to talk about the project. I'm fortunate to have a body of work that speaks for itself and don't need to audition anymore.

"Did I get it?" I ask.

"You got it!"

I cheer and do a little happy dance in my seat while Will goes over the terms of my contract. I'm barely paying attention, knowing Will has my back, when he says, "Small hiccup. The production schedule creates a conflict with *The Highlighter*. I can get you out of your contract with them, and then it's full steam ahead." *The Highlighter* is the indie movie I was set to film in Vancouver in less than two weeks.

And I convinced Owen to go with me for a job with their studio. Shit. I can't let my career screw things up with Owen again. Things are going so well.

"Will, I can't leave Craig and Darla in the lurch like this." That's the producer and director of *The Highlighter*.

And I can't leave Owen in the lurch either.

"They'll find someone else."

"It's less than two weeks."

"Shayla, I know you want to do this little indie film for the street cred, but there will be other indie films. You can do a dozen of them after you land this whale. Nala is a once-in-a-lifetime role. It has franchise potential. I'm talking sequels, a world of interconnected films, comic books, video games, merchandise. You'll be a role model to little girls all over the world."

That gets me. I want girls to own their power, especially

since I felt so powerless as a little girl with my controlling mother and working with adults in the industry.

"I would hate to miss out on this project," I say.

"You're making the right decision. Let me hammer out the details with Spotlight Pictures, and I'll get back to you when it's official. And I'm sure I don't need to remind you of the importance of secrecy while I work my magic on this end. Don't share your news with a soul, got it?"

I hesitate. I really want to tell Owen. I need to explain the change of plans and that he probably won't have a job with the indie film studio.

"Shayla?"

"Can I just tell my boyfriend?"

"No one."

"Got it."

"Oh, and filming will be in LA, so you can settle in back at home. I'd love to take you to lunch when you get here."

"Sure, but, uh, do you think Craig and Darla will hold it against me?"

"Shayla, you're going to be so big after this, no one can afford to hold a grudge. You'll be gold. Everyone's going to want you, even Craig and Darla."

"I'd like to send them a note, saying I hope we can work together again. Oh, I might have the perfect replacement. My friend Vanessa Billings just ended a long run on a sitcom and might like to try an indie film to show off her versatility. I'll get in touch with her."

"That's fine, just wait until you get the all clear from me. I'd like to make this happen without a lawsuit. You just focus on Nala. I'm going to send you over the latest version of the script. Congratulations, Shayla, I'm thrilled for you. Do something nice for yourself. This is a major win."

He hangs up. I sit there a few moments, my mind reeling. I'll be in LA again. Maybe I could offer Owen an all-expenses-paid three-month trip to LA. That way he'd know how much I want to stay together no matter where my job takes me. I so hope everything works out.

I had the Oliver Nuckowski project in the back of my mind, but there were some financing hurdles, and I thought it would be years before it got the backing it needed, if it did at all. I can't believe I got Nala. This is *everything*.

I tap over to my email to read the latest script.

~

Owen

Shayla and I had a fantastic weekend together. She was in a good mood, and it rubbed off on me. We had Mackenzie, Harper, and Olivia over on Friday night for dinner. I invited Nathan too, but he had a date. On Saturday night, Shayla and I had a movie marathon, mostly sci-fi and fantasy, which I like, and we spent the rest of the time in bed. I could get used to this.

I sit at the kitchen table with a glass of water and my laptop. If this is what our life would be like, right here in Clover Park, I'd say yes to us in a heartbeat. It's Monday night, and I find myself excited for her to walk in the door so we can have dinner together. Takeout's waiting on the counter.

I take a drink of water. Does looking forward to the small things like dinner on a Monday mean I'm in love with Shayla? Adrenaline fires through me at the thought. With risk comes reward, right?

The front door opens, and Shayla calls, "Owen Campbell! Where's my welcome-back hug?"

I stride to the foyer, grab her in a hug, and swing her around. She laughs. I put her down, take one look at her happy glowing face, and my heart cracks open. I love her. There's no sense denying it anymore.

I kiss her. "You hungry? I got meatloaf and potatoes from Happy Endings."

"Please tell me you got something with vegetables too."

"And I got you veggie loaf with cauliflower rice. Blech. I always wondered who ordered from the healthy menu."

We head to the kitchen. I get the containers out of the bag while Shayla sets the table. We make a good team.

At dinner, Shayla tells me the latest on set. I know everyone from my stint as her guard, so it's fun to hear. I tell her about an interesting job I worked this week at a tech company that believed they had a mole leaking company secrets through the dark web. I found her within an hour, the seventeen-year-old daughter of the CEO. Some daughter-daddy issues there.

After we finish eating, she says brightly, "I have good news."

I smile. "Yeah, what is it?"

"You're looking at the new star of the next Oliver Nuckowski film. It's a great role. Nala is this kickass woman on a quest. She's just everything. It's set in a fantasy world that's like an ecotopia. No pollution, everything runs on clean energy. I just read the latest script, and it's even better than the first version I read. My agent says it has franchise potential. I'll be a role model to girls all over the world."

"Congratulations! That's amazing!"

I walk around the table to hug her. She leaps to her feet and throws herself in my arms. I give her a kiss and go back to my seat.

"Is that why we had a sci-fi and fantasy movie marathon this weekend?" I ask.

She laughs. "Yes. I couldn't say anything until it was official. It was so hard not to tell you, but my agent said it could jeopardize the deal."

"I wouldn't have said anything to anyone."

"I guess I was afraid to go against what he said. Anyway, now you know."

"Where does it film?"

"LA."

"I guess that's better than Australia." I can't begrudge her a major role that she's excited about. "How long will you be away?"

"A little over three months. I'd love to have you with me.

All expenses paid of course. I'm not sure I can get you a job with this studio, but we could be together."

"I can't leave for three months. I have work. I'll be with you in Vancouver, but I can't keep following you from set to set." I can feel my heart creaking closed again. This was the elephant in the room neither one of us wanted to acknowledge.

"Actually, the Vancouver project was cancelled."

I still. No Vancouver job. No DC job. Shit.

"Why?" I ask.

"I had to get out of my contract to do this other project. It starts filming after the Fourth of July. Oliver was able to assemble everyone he needed ahead of time. His crew often follow him from project to project. He got the financing, and it's a go."

I frown. "So you're telling me you pulled out of the Vancouver project that you said would give me a job and is the whole reason I lost the DC job? This is really going to hurt my company's bottom line. Why wasn't I included in this decision? At least we could've talked about it. How long have you known?"

"It was just official today."

I clench my jaw. "When did you unofficially find out about this?"

"Friday. But my agent swore me to secrecy. It was a delicate situation. We were trying to avoid a lawsuit."

"You could've trusted me."

"Okay, I see now that I probably should've mentioned it earlier, but I don't see what difference that would have made. I have to take this project, which means I have to drop the other one. You understand how important this role is, right? I could show you the script." She goes for her phone.

I grab it and put it facedown on the table. "You dangle a job in front of me; then it's gone. I imagine the Vancouver people are pretty pissed you pulled out at the last minute. You think they're going to want to hire the guy you recommended now?"

She's quiet for a long moment. "Okay, I get why you're upset, but I hoped my offer of a three-month all-expenses-paid trip to LA would make up for it a little. I don't want work to get between us again."

"Well, it did. And you can't buy me off with a trip."

"I'm sorry." She stares at her plate and mutters, "I feel like I'm always apologizing to you."

That pisses me off. "And I'm tired of hearing it." I push my plate back. "You're still lying to me, Shay, acting like nothing changed when you had this major news that affects me too. We were together all weekend, and you could've said something at any time."

"That's not a lie!"

"It's a lie of omission. And you lied when you said you'd stay in touch. Instead you stayed in touch with my sister, my cousin, Mom, everyone around me, but not me. Let's leave Owen in the dark. He'll just go along."

She huffs. "Are you going to bring up our past every time you're mad at me? How many times can I apologize for not staying in touch when I was sixteen years old on the brink of my big break? And this is not a lie. I do have a bigger, better job thanks to my agent. This Vancouver film was for an indie darling. They can replace me easily, in fact I already found someone for the role, and after this Oliver Nuckowski film, I'll have my choice of projects."

I go cold. Once again, it's all about her and her career. Who cares who gets shut out as a result?

"Why can't you just be happy for me?" she asks.

I stand. "I'm out."

"You're going out?"

"I mean I'm out because we're over. Pack your things. I don't want to see you when I get back."

I storm toward the door, but I still hear her yell, "Owen, please! Let's talk about this."

I stop without turning around. "Text Zander before you leave!"

As soon as I get outside, I run, adrenaline racing through

me. I don't need this. I was fine before she swept into town, and I'll be fine when she leaves.

When I finally wear myself out, I find myself at the Happy Endings bar. The worst of my anger has passed, replaced by the sting of betrayal. I can't trust her. She thinks she can just yank me out of my life and change the plan whenever it suits her with no regard for what I want.

And then she dangles a three-month trip in front of me like I can be bought. Screw that. I'm not impressed with the glamour of Hollywood. I grew up on movie sets.

My cousin Cooper is behind the bar tonight. His light brown hair is rumpled as usual, his jaw scruffy. "Hey, cuz. Is this a beer night or whisky?"

I meet his sympathetic brown eyes. He can read people like a book, or maybe I just look as bad as I feel. "Whisky."

He turns to get it.

I lean on the bar top and rest my head in my hands, suddenly exhausted. A few moments later, a tumbler of whiskey slides across the bar to me. I take a sip.

Cooper dries some glasses under the bar. "Wanna talk to your friendly neighborhood bartender about it? Monday nights are brutally slow, so I've got all the time in the world."

I stare at the amber whiskey. "No."

"Let me guess, you had a fight with Shayla, and she told you to sleep on the couch tonight."

I lift my gaze. "What part of *I don't want to talk about it* don't you understand?"

"You might be older than me—"

"Not that much older," I mutter. Only three years.

He continues as if I haven't spoken. "But I've packed a lot of experience in there. I've had multiple relationships."

"You rescue women. Of course they stick with you. It's hero worship."

"I do like to be adored. Probably helps that I have a sister, so I understand women."

"So do I."

"True, but somehow you missed the part where you understand what women want."

I rub my beard, debating leaving. I didn't come here for Cooper to wax philosophical on women where he looks like the hero and I look like an idiot.

He leans an elbow on the bar top. "From what I heard, you haven't been with anyone serious since Shayla."

"So? I like keeping things casual."

"Mackenzie says Shayla moved in with you."

I toss some whisky back. "That was for her safety." *Did she text Zander to come get her after I left?*

Not my concern.

Cooper waxes philosophic once more. "Me, if I had a woman like Shayla Adler, I wouldn't let her go. She's beautiful, talented, smart, and generous." He taps the bar top. "She bought her friends a house."

I finish my whisky, the burn going straight to my gut. "You can have her."

He shoves my shoulder. "Nah, you're too hung up on her."

I push my tumbler toward him. "Shut up and pour."

I ended it on my terms. I have a job, friends, family. *Here.* It was a mistake to let her in. I won't let that happen again.

16

———————

Shayla

I pack my suitcases in a hurry and walk out of Owen's house with my head held high. I've done nothing wrong. I can't discuss projects until the official word goes out. And I'm sorry he lost a job over it, I really am. That was not my intention.

I push open the front door and struggle to get my two large wheeled suitcases out while balancing my purse and a tote. Finally, I manage it and just stand there on his porch. I turn and consider going back in. I wanted to include him in my big news. Maybe if I had…

No. Everyone knows you can't blab about a deal until it's final. There was real risk to this project with the delicate negotiation to get me out of my previous project.

I march down the sidewalk, back to a righteous fury, my suitcases bumping along behind me. God, these are heavy. Maybe I should've texted Zander. No, I can do this myself. It's only a block to my house.

How can our relationship ever move forward when Owen keeps bringing up the past? I can't change the past. And I've apologized *many times*.

A car slows to drive alongside me. I give it a sideways

glance, a beige sedan. My heart races, and I walk faster. *Please don't let it be Matt.*

The car keeps up with me.

I break into a cold sweat, debating my options. I could hit him with my tote. I could run. Which direction? No one's home at Owen's house. Where's the police station again?

The car speeds ahead of me and parks. The driver's side door opens and slams shut.

I do an about-face, heading back to Owen's house as fast as I can.

"Shayla!" a male voice calls. "Can I give you a ride somewhere?"

I stop. That voice sounds familiar. I turn to see Owen's cousin Finn and nearly collapse in relief.

He grins as he approaches. "Like my new car? Well, it's new to me. Olivia paid me overtime to finish painting faster."

I bite back a smile. I let her increase his pay at her sincere request. She couldn't handle a gorgeous younger man taking an interest in her. That's not in her five-year world-domination plan.

He takes my suitcases from me, lifting them like they weigh nothing. "Where you headed?"

I point to my house down the block. "Home."

"Guess you're done living with Owen."

"Afraid so."

"Wait until you see your place. The crown molding really pops against the new colors on the walls. You're going to love it."

"I'm sure I will."

"Aren't you supposed to be with your bodyguard?"

I pat his shoulder. "You'll do just fine."

His chest puffs out. "I am a black belt. Mom was worried about me going to college in the big scary city, so Dad got me into krav maga a couple of summers ago too. Part of my street-smarts education."

"You're lucky to have parents like that to guide you. And nice siblings too."

"Yeah, they're great. Too bad Cooper is so damn annoying, still playing the big-brother card. I'm a frigging adult now. If they can draft me, then I can make my own decisions."

"Oh, come on. What'd he do that's so bad?"

"Always giving advice. And you'd think he'd invented getting with a woman. I hope he meets a woman who knocks him on his ass. Not literally. You know what I mean."

I smile despite my current state of angst over Owen. It's hard not to smile around Finn. "That doesn't sound too bad to me."

He shoots me a look.

"I mean how annoying."

"Right?"

We arrive at my house. I send a quick text to Olivia that I'm here and why. *Moving back in because it's over with Owen.* I don't want to startle her by opening the door when everyone's always on alert for an unexpected visitor.

I glance around behind me. Coast is clear. Finn smiles at me encouragingly. I open the door with my key.

Zander and Olivia are in the front room, and they don't look happy.

Finn brings my luggage in. "Hi, Olivia." His voice sounds warm and inviting.

"Hi." She turns to me. "At least Finn was with you. Did you call him?"

"No, I just ran into him on my way here."

Finn waves bye and leaves.

I step farther into the room and sigh. "This room does look good. Brighter with the light yellow walls and white crown molding."

"Shayla!" Olivia says. "Do you know how valuable you are? You can't take chances like that."

For a moment, it feels like Olivia is mothering me. I guess she really cares.

"You should've let me know you were alone," Zander says. "That's what I'm here for."

"I know, I'm sorry. It was only a block, and I was upset."

Olivia glances at the suitcases. "Sorry about Owen. I guess it's good your film wraps in a week. We can get back to LA."

I swallow over the lump of emotion lodged in my throat.

Footsteps thunder down the stairs. "I thought I heard your voice," Harper says. She looks back toward the upstairs. "Mac, Shayla's here."

"Harp! Mac is a truck!"

Harper smiles. "I actually don't mind Harp."

Mackenzie appears at the top of the stairs, takes one look at me and my suitcases, and says, "This looks like a wine and chocolate situation."

My lower lip quivers. I nod.

Harper and Mackenzie join me a moment later and fold me into a group hug.

"Olivia!" I call. "Get in here!"

Olivia joins the hug.

Zander clears his throat. "I'll take these suitcases up to your room."

"Thank you," I say.

We pull away from the hug. Mackenzie gives me a sympathetic look.

"He kicked me out," I say. "I love him with all my heart, and he kicked me out." My face crumples, tears falling in earnest. "I screwed up, and I wanted so much for this to work out."

Olivia produces a tissue and hands it to me. I wipe my tears. "Thanks."

She gestures for me to follow her to the kitchen. We all file in behind her. Oh, they added a square light wood table and chairs in one corner. That looks like a cozy spot.

Mackenzie gestures to the table. "Sit. I'll get the chocolate."

"I'll get the wine," Harper says.

"I'll get napkins and glasses," Olivia says.

I take a seat, humbled by their support. I haven't spent much time with them between Owen and work. Well, now they're both ending. My throat tightens. "It's so good to see you all again."

"Back at ya." Harper uncorks a bottle of white wine. "This is a Loire Valley sauvignon blanc. Please take the time to savor it during this difficult time."

"Better get a backup bottle too," Olivia says, setting napkins and glasses on each place setting. "There are four of us."

"Okay, but we can't start with the backup bottle," Harper says. "Mackenzie got it from the sale section."

Mackenzie takes a seat adjacent to me. "Just because it's on sale doesn't mean it's not good."

Harper joins us and pours me a generous glass. "It had dust on the bottle. That means nobody wanted it."

"Wine gets better with age," Mackenzie says.

Harper holds the sauvignon blanc bottle above Mackenzie's glass without pouring. "Does that mean you'd prefer the sale stuff?"

Mackenzie points to her glass, looking contrite.

Harper pours. "Thought so."

After we all have our wine, Harper lifts her glass in a toast. "To kickass women."

I stare at my glass. "I don't feel very kickass at the moment, more like devastated, hurt, angry, and sad. So sad."

The women stare at me.

"We can't drink until we all toast," Harper says.

I lift my glass and clink glasses with everyone.

"So what'd my brother do?" Harper asks me.

I straighten, happy she's taking my side. "He got mad at me and kicked me out. And I quote, 'Pack your bags.'"

"So sorry," Mackenzie says, rubbing my arm.

Olivia nods and sips her wine.

"Any reason you'd like to share?" Harper asks.

I launch into the whole story, starting with my great new project that I couldn't tell him about until it was official, the end of the Vancouver job, my offer of a paid three-month trip, and the fact that Owen hasn't forgiven me for the past.

"I guess I have to take some responsibility," I say. "I should've just told him how much I love him and want a future with him, but I was afraid to scare him off. And the truth is, I wanted him to be with me no matter what. I never should've made it about a job for both of us, right? I should've just said, Owen, I love you and want us to be together whether it's in Clover Park, Vancouver, or LA. Home is with you."

Silence.

"Right?"

"Well…" Harper says.

"Are you sure he felt the same way?" Mackenzie asks gently.

"I thought so." I hesitate. "It felt that way. Do you think I was imagining it?"

"No, he was into you," Olivia says with a note of authority. "That much is clear. Uproot-his-life level of into you, that I'm not sure about."

"Your mom made it work with your dad," I say to Harper. "She made me think anything was possible."

Harper considers that. "Mom always discussed projects with Dad before it was official. It was just understood they were in this together, and it had to work with both of their schedules."

"But my agent said—"

Harper cuts me off. "Is your agent the guy you want a future with?"

I glance at Mackenzie for backup, but she looks like she's agreeing with Harper. "Well, yeah, but not that way. I guess I never had a serious relationship before when I was faced with a big career decision." I smack my forehead. "Except the first time I was in a serious relationship with Owen. No wonder he can't forgive me."

"I don't think you can call a relationship when you were teens serious," Mackenzie says. "You were just too young for a commitment."

I'm about to protest that we *were* serious when she adds, "Even if the feelings between you were the real thing."

I look around the table, hoping for support with my idea to fix things. "I offered him an all-expenses-paid trip for three months to LA so we could stay together, and he rejected it. He accused me of buying him off. I just wanted us to be together."

"Sounds like manly pride," Olivia says.

Harper tilts her head. "Maybe. I can see both sides. The need for discretion, and the need to include your significant other in life choices that affect both of you."

"He's probably pissed about losing the Vancouver job since it screwed up his DC job too," Olivia points out oh-so-helpfully.

"The DC client was being inflexible," Mackenzie says. "I've got other potential jobs lined up. We'll be fine."

"Yeah, but she did dangle a major job in front of him," Harper says. She turns to me. "And then your career took precedence over his with no discussion."

Tears threaten. "I thought you were on my side," I say in a small voice.

"I'm on both your sides," Harper says.

Mackenzie shrugs. "He is family."

Stung, I can feel myself withdrawing. I'd hoped we were like family too. Didn't they say we were honorary sisters?

"This is a good career move for you, Shayla," Olivia says. "All you can do is look forward."

I finish my wine in one long swallow. "I'm going back to the hotel in the city."

"No," Mackenzie says. "Stay here with us."

I shake my head. "I'm putting you at risk, and honestly, I need a break from reminders of Owen. The resemblance here is just too much." *And the fact that you're on his side.*

"I don't look that much like him, do I?" Harper asks, turning to Mackenzie.

"Yeah, around the eyes and cheekbones," Mackenzie says. "Your nose too."

"You do too," Harper says.

"Makes sense," Mackenzie says. "Twin Campbell genes. It's almost like genetically we had the same dad."

I leave them to their discussion of genes and how closely they really are related. All I know is I'm not family. They'll always side with Owen. Blood is thicker than water, blah, blah, blah.

I need to burrow into my safe hotel room cocoon. Alone once more. Maybe that's how I'll always be. Tears sting my eyes, and I hurry from the room.

I drag myself through my last week at work. I've never been so depressed in my life. Losing Owen feels like a double loss. All the emotions from losing him in the past and the present mixing together to make for a toxic soup of regret, pain, and sadness. I'd held out hope for so long. Now it's dead just like our relationship.

I know now I should've included him in decisions that affect both our futures. Maybe he would've joined me in LA, or maybe he wouldn't, but the three-month separation might've been okay if he knew I made him a priority. Given our past, it was a tricky road to navigate. I hurt him once, and that made this time around so much worse. I can see it from his side. What I can't see is how to fix this. Maybe it's too late. Maybe he doesn't believe we have a future anymore, and that's why he won't talk to me. He's making a clean break.

Olivia booked us on a flight back to LA on the same day filming wrapped. Not a moment too soon. I've been holding myself together with sheer grit. We left Zander behind in favor of hiring a guard in LA. It's fine. There haven't been any incidents with Matt in weeks. Only my imagination, seeing him out of the corner of my eye. I can't let him into my head because then he wins.

I settle into my first-class seat and proceed to work my way through a share-size bag of peanut M&M's.

Olivia nudges my arm. "It says share right on the bag."

I offer her some, though I don't want to. "I should've swiped a bag for you too."

She pours a handful of candy for herself. "Where'd you get these?"

"Craft services."

"I'll never understand how craft services can offer junk food when stars are expected to be fit and not gain an ounce on the job."

"I have four weeks until my next project starts. Can you just let me wallow in sugar, please?"

"Of course." She puts her M&M's back in the bag, one by one. "Don't worry. I don't have germs."

It's kinda gross, but I don't care. I need sugar right now.

I finish the bag just in time for takeoff and look out the window, watching New York getting smaller and smaller in the distance. I imagine I can see the corner of Connecticut next to southern New York. Goodbye, Clover Park; goodbye, fake sisters; goodbye, heartbreaker. My eyes get hot, my throat tight. A tear escapes.

"You're going to be okay," Olivia says firmly.

I turn to her. "How do you know?"

"Because you're strong."

"I am?"

"Obviously. I know it's not easy to put in the long hours you do while dealing with the pressures of fame and some downright dangerous situations."

"Claire taught me how to keep the right perspective, and guards help with dangerous situations. I don't do any of this on my own."

"You show up and you work hard, even when you're hurting. Trust me, you're strong."

I give her a small smile. "You too. I'm impressed with your organizational skills and your planning. I'm sure you won't be with me for long."

She sighs and leans her head back on the seat. "Clover

Park was an interesting experience. Still, I'll be glad to get back to LA."

"Are you going to keep in touch with Finn?"

"I told him he could text me to let me know how his studies are going."

"That's it? His studies?"

"Shayla, he's nineteen. Still a boy."

"He seemed mature and sweet too."

She puts her cushioned headphones on. "Yeah, well, he'll have to be mature and sweet to someone in college." She cues up her music on her phone.

"So why keep in touch?"

She doesn't answer, already listening to her music. I wave in front of her face.

She lifts a headphone cushion off one ear. "Yeah?"

"Why keep in touch?"

"I keep in touch with everyone I meet. Hollywood is all about connections." She drops her headphone back in place.

But Finn's not part of Hollywood. I let it go. Who knows, maybe one day he'll be useful to her, or vice versa. At least that's the way Olivia sees the world.

I pick up my phone, checking for texts or missed calls from Owen. Pathetic, I know. The moment we broke up, it was like I no longer existed for him.

I hate to admit it, but my first night back at the hotel in the city, I couldn't sleep and ended up texting him late at night. *Can we talk?*

I so wish I could take that text back. Obviously, his answer is no.

17

Owen

"Okay, Owen, we all know you're heartbroken, but can you stop taking it out on us?" Nathan asks at our work meeting the Friday after Shayla left for LA. How do I know she left? I got in touch with Zander to make sure he was staying on with her after filming wrapped, and guess what? He's not. She let him go in favor of hiring someone in LA. And how long will that take?

"I'm fine," I snap. "What's next for business? I'll take it."

"Owen," Mackenzie says gently, "we already covered that. Nathan's taking the biotech job in New Jersey. You're up for whatever comes next. We're having a lull with the Fourth of July holiday coming up. Why don't you take some time off?"

"And do what?"

Nathan and Mackenzie exchange a look.

"What?" I bark.

"We think you should go to LA and check in with Shayla," Mackenzie says. "Talk things through."

Nathan nods vigorously.

I exhale sharply. "And what's that going to solve? She puts everyone and everything ahead of me. So I'm just supposed to trail after her wherever she goes? No, thanks."

Mackenzie gives me a sympathetic look. "You know the

first time she left for a job when she was sixteen, she was in a tough place."

"I know her mom was hard on her," I mutter.

"It was emotional abuse, constant criticism about her looks and her weight, constant comparison to other girls who were doing better than her in their careers. Her self-esteem was destroyed. She'd just become an emancipated minor when you met her, so she was flying without a net for the first time, sixteen years old and trying to make a life for herself. She had to take that job."

And she was dealing with Hollywood, which can chew up young girls. Not to mention she'd recently given up drugs and alcohol, her coping mechanism. She was alone in a tough industry doing the best she could to make sure she landed on a good path.

And I hated her for that. Guilt stabs at me. I only thought about my side of things. Selfish. She had stuff to deal with and made the only decision that made sense at the time and, in fact, gave her the successful career she has today.

I proposed back then, but I shouldn't have. She was still fighting for her life. And I wasn't the man I am today. It wouldn't have worked out back then, but now? I still don't see how to make a future work for both of us.

"Do you love her?" Mackenzie asks.

"Thought you didn't believe in love," I return.

"I do, just not for me at this time," Mackenzie says.

"What time are you waiting for?" Nathan asks.

She gives him a small smile. "I'll know when I'm ready. For now I just want to have fun."

"Me too," Nathan says.

I grunt. "We've got to get more business. I'll do some cold-calling."

Mackenzie clicks on her laptop. "Sure, I'll email you the list I was working on. You might not get a hold of a number of these, though. People do like to take vacation time around now. Kids are out of school. It's warm outside—"

"The Fourth," I say. "I get it. Just give it to me."

"Okay, okay," Mackenzie says, not looking up from her laptop. "There. It's yours."

"Thank you," I bite out.

Nathan leans back in his seat and props his feet on the table. "You know what your problem is, Owen?"

"I don't have a problem."

"You fall in love too easily. You should be more like me. Just ride it out until it's not exciting anymore and move on."

I send him a dark look, not bothering to justify that stupidity with a response. Besides, I'm no longer in love with Shayla. I've forgiven her for the past, but that doesn't mean we have a future. Nothing's really changed.

My gut churns. She texted me, asking to talk, and I ignored it.

"He's only ever loved one woman," Mackenzie says to Nathan. She turns to me. "And she loves you too, even after you kicked her out." She slaps a hand over her mouth. "Oops."

"Oops," I echo, sitting up straighter. "She said that?"

"I can neither confirm nor deny," Mackenzie says.

"She used to love me," I clarify.

"Just get on a fucking plane and find out," Nathan says.

I stand abruptly and grab my laptop. "I'm not going to LA to patch things up. I just need to check on her security setup since she let Zander go."

"Oh my God, she didn't take Zander?" Mackenzie exclaims. "I didn't know that. Go, go, go! She needs you."

I bolt out the door. Mackenzie's right. Shayla needs me for her own protection.

I walk into Shayla's house through the open patio door, every nerve ending at attention. She wouldn't be so careless as to leave the door open. I checked in with Olivia earlier, and there's no bodyguard yet. Shayla lives alone on a private lot.

I approach the kitchen and hear a man's voice. I halt, my heart kicking harder.

"Katie, I'm glad we can be alone again."

Adrenaline fires through me. I carefully shift to get a better look. Yup. It's Matt. He's obsessed with the teenaged runaway character Shayla played, Katie, who turned to prostitution to survive. He must've deactivated the security system somehow. I should've come out here with her and made sure she had a tamperproof system. Damn my stupid pride.

Matt sits on a stool at the kitchen island. Shayla stands frozen in place by the refrigerator in her robe, closer to him than me.

She must've come down for breakfast and been surprised by him. I'm not sure if he has a weapon. I wait, hoping Shayla will move out of the danger zone long enough for me to take Matt down.

He smiles at her. You'd never know he was dangerous just looking at him. He looks like a friendly neighbor with neat brown hair parted to the side and black rectangular-framed glasses.

Shayla backs up a step. *Yes, come this way.*

"Don't leave," Matt says. "I came all this way to see you."

"What do you want?"

"I just want to be with you, Katie." He sets a wad of crumpled dollar bills on the counter. "I brought cash. I can afford you."

Damn his sick mind.

"How did you get in here?" she asks in a shaky voice.

He laughs. "You didn't even notice the power went off while you were sleeping. That's the advantage of thinking ahead. Your security system was laughably easy to shut down."

Shayla takes another step back, and he pulls out a gun. My stomach drops. *No! It's not going to end this way.*

"Don't go," he says. "This can be nice and easy."

She clears her throat and offers him a sunny smile.

"Would you like breakfast? I was just about to make pancakes."

Yes, distract him and move out of the way.

He sets the gun on the island. "I didn't know you could cook, Katie. I might have to hire you for the long term. I'll call you my companion. Prostitute is such a hard word, don't you agree?"

She shifts farther away, going to the pantry and taking out a box of pancake mix. I'm about to make my move when she saunters right up to him and rubs his arm. "I like to play a game with my guests. It's called guess what kind of pancakes I make. You get to be blindfolded and just guess by scent and taste. Would you like to play?"

"Sounds kinky."

She gives him a sexy smile, her acting skills paying off. "It can be. But it'll cost you extra."

"I can afford it. Trust me, there's more where that came from."

"Good," she croons as she pulls a dark red cloth napkin from a drawer. She trails a finger across his shoulder as she steps behind him. The moment he's blindfolded, I'm stepping in.

He turns and smashes his lips against hers. Too damn close. I fight back the rage. I need to make sure she's at a safe distance.

He pulls back. "That was just a preview."

"Mmm-hmm."

He grabs his gun and holds it between them.

"I'm just going to step behind you to put this on." She puts the blindfold on him and ties it in the back. "Can you see anything?"

"Nope."

"Would you mind putting the gun down? It's hard for me to focus on our game."

He sets it on the island but keeps his hand on it. I crouch down, planning on sneaking up behind him.

She goes to the refrigerator and starts taking out ingredients.

"Is it blueberries?" he asks.

"No, it's more exotic than that. I bet you'll never guess it."

He giggles. "I can't wait to taste you."

You will pay, asshole.

I make my way to the island, coming around the corner to where he's seated. I rise to my feet just as Shayla swings a large cast-iron pan at his head.

He stumbles out of his seat. I see the glint of light reflecting off his gun and charge, taking him down. His blindfold pops off in the scuffle.

He struggles to aim the gun at me, and I slam his wrist back against the ceramic tile, causing the gun to shake loose.

We dive for it at the same time. I grab it first. He tries to kick me in the nuts, and I block and counter with a swift punch to the nose. Blood spurts out, and he howls.

I stick the gun in the back of my jeans, twist his arms behind his back, and hold him down over the island counter.

I meet Shayla's huge eyes for the first time. "Call the police. He's going to jail this time."

She dashes upstairs.

Jesus, her phone is all the way up there? What if I hadn't shown up this morning? I can't bear the thought of anything happening to her. I need her to be safe and well. I need her in my life.

"Katie, don't go," Matt says.

I slam his head on the island, knocking him unconscious. Then I drop him on the floor and tie him there with some kitchen string. It won't hold for long once he wakes, but I'll keep him in his place.

No one messes with my woman.

～

Shayla

The moment the police take Matt away, I rush into Owen's open arms.

I look up at him, my arms tucked around his middle. "What are you doing here? And how did you get in?"

He brushes my hair back from my face. "The back patio door was open, and I'm here because—"

"You missed me."

He sighs so big it parts my hair. "I told everyone I was going to check on your security system, but when I saw you alone facing Matt, I—" his voice chokes "—I can't bear to think of not having you in my life. I love you, Shayla, I always have and always will."

Tears sting my eyes. I said the same thing to him not long ago, and now he's returning that love. "I love you too. I've missed you so much. You were the one who didn't keep in touch this time."

"Because I was stupidly trying to get over you. Impossible. And I understand now about the pressure you were under when we were together the first time. I forgive you, and I hope you can forgive me for being so selfish and only seeing my side."

My heart soars. He's finally putting the past behind us. "Of course I forgive you. Are we really doing this?"

"We're really doing this, but I have some rules. We have to talk about stuff that affects both of us."

I nod solemnly. "Harper told me how your mom brings your dad in on everything before it's official. I guess I never had a serious relationship before. It didn't occur to me."

"Me either, besides you. I guess we're each other's serious relationship."

I kiss him. "You were my first. I hope you'll be my last."

He grins. "Shayla Adler, are you proposing to me?"

"That depends on your answer."

He crushes me to his chest. We stay like that for long moments. Me crushed by love; Owen considering my proposal. I'll wait as long as I have to for his answer. He sure waited a long time for mine.

He pulls back. "God, Shayla, I thought I'd lost you forever. I've never been so terrified in my life as when I saw that open door and found you in the kitchen with him. As far as I'm concerned, you're stuck with me for life."

"So that's a yes? Wait. Let me make it official. Owen Campbell, will you marry me?"

"Absolutely."

I bounce on the balls of my feet, happiness bubbling up inside me. "I'll get you a ring."

"And I'll get you one too."

He bends me over his arm and kisses me just like in the movies. I love it, and I love him. Always.

Just like I told him all those years ago.

EPILOGUE

Three months later…

I signed the deed of my Clover Park house over to my honorary sisters, Harper and Mackenzie. They plan to live there together. Maybe down the line they'll sell it and split the proceeds, but for now they're my neighbors. Yup, I moved into Owen's house in Clover Park. While I was in LA, Owen came out every other weekend to visit me. We're making it work.

As for the future, we're going to talk about all projects that come up for each of us and make sure it's good for us as a couple. I'll be working closely with Claire's production company, Red Jewel Films, and hopefully be in some films that are filmed locally. It's important to me and Owen that we're close to his family, whom I love almost as much as I love him.

Now we're on our way to Happy Endings for our engagement party. It's mid-October and raining. Owen insisted on driving us, even though we live just a couple of blocks away because he didn't want my dress or shoes to get ruined in the rain. He's so thoughtful that way. My guard Zander is already there. I hired a second guard to give Zander breaks, who's also willing to travel with me. Harry's a hulk of a man who used to work for a rock star until his client got into drugs. Harry has a strict no-drug policy, which works for me.

Owen parks and cups the back of my neck, drawing me close for a kiss. "You look beautiful. Are you ready for the mob scene in there?"

I laugh. "It's not a mob scene. Believe me, I've experienced those. It's just your family, who I love."

"And they love you too."

"Good."

"Stay right there."

He gets out of the car and walks around to my side, umbrella in hand.

I smooth out the bottom of my black dress. The dress is new. Long sleeves with a cutout on top to show off my cleavage, which by the way is not huge, but it's still flattering. The bottom ends mid-thigh. I paired it with strappy black heels. Owen's wearing a charcoal gray suit with no tie.

He opens my door and helps me out, holding the umbrella over me. He shuts the door behind me.

I rub his chest. "Looking mighty handsome in your suit, Mr. Campbell."

"Looking mighty beautiful in your dress, future Mrs. Campbell."

"Uh, I'm actually not taking your name for professional reasons."

"I know, but I'll think of you as Mrs. Campbell anyway."

"You're surprisingly old-fashioned."

"You take that back." He hands me the umbrella and then shocks me by sweeping me off my feet in his romantic way.

"What're you doing!"

He starts walking toward the back door of Happy Endings. "I'm going to carry you over the threshold."

"Isn't that what you do *after* you're married?"

"I don't know. I didn't check with Aunt Hailey on the proper wedding protocol. By the way, she has a wedding today across the street at Ludbury House, but she says she should be able to pop in to congratulate us."

"Let's have our wedding in Clover Park with Hailey running it. Ludbury House is beautiful."

"I'm glad you said it first because I know she'd be crushed if we didn't let her help plan it. That's actually where my parents got married."

I rub his chest. "I know, and they're still happily married."

"I have to warn you, Hailey is a force."

"So am I."

He sets me down by the back door. "No, seriously."

"Owen, I can handle her just like I handle you."

His large hand cradles my jaw. "Oh, you handle me, do you?" He lowers his head, his lips meeting mine in a tender kiss.

I drop the umbrella, grab his head, and kiss him again, all of my love and affection pouring into a long passionate kiss.

When we break apart, I spot Zander on the other side of the door, his head turned away for privacy.

"I think we just gave Zander an eyeful," I say, picking up the umbrella. "Hey, the rain stopped." I close it and set it against the side of the building.

"Zander will have to get used to it." He scoops me up, and I squeal in surprise.

"I thought we were done with this part!"

"Shh, I'm carrying you over the threshold. You're going to alarm the family with your screams."

"It wasn't a scream. It was a small sound of surprise."

He carries me over the threshold and sets me down, taking my hand as we enter the dining area of the restaurant. The place is decorated with silver, gold, and white streamers, lots of cheerful bobbing silver and gold balloons, and a large banner that says Congratulations Owen and Shayla!

"Congratulations!" our family and friends shout.

Claire runs over to hug us both, and then clips a small veil to my hair. "So everyone knows who the bride is. Hope you don't mind there's going to be lots of pictures. Strictly for family."

"That would be great," I say.

"Good." She kisses my cheek. "I'm so glad you're joining the family. Now I can truly claim you as my daughter."

My eyes get hot. "I already claimed you as Mom, so that works."

She squeezes my arm. "Aww. Come on, everyone's here except Hailey. She'll be here soon, I hope." She gestures to an enlarged picture on an easel. "What do you think?"

My lips part in surprise. I've never seen this picture before. It's me and Owen as teens by the pool, wrapped in a single towel, smiling at each other.

"I love it!"

"Who took this picture?" Owen asks.

"Who else? Our resident photographer."

"Rafael?"

Rafael walks over. "Yes?"

"You took this picture?" Owen asks. "You must've been thirteen. You'd just gotten your first camera for Christmas."

"You like it?"

"It's amazing. You captured a moment here."

I gesture to it. "You captured emotion, our bond."

Rafael smiles. "Yeah, well, anyone with eyes could've seen what you two had."

I hug him. "If you have any other sneak pictures of us, I'd love to see them."

"Oh dear God," Owen says. "I shudder to think about what you might've seen. What a sneak you were."

"Nothing X-rated, if that's what you're worried about," he says.

"I sure hope not," Claire says. "Shayla was under our supervision."

Owen and I exchange an amused look.

"I'll give you what I have as a wedding present," Rafael says.

I turn to Owen. "Isn't he full of surprises?"

Claire looks thoughtful. "I wonder what other pictures thirteen-year-old Rafael took around the house on the down-low. I'd better look into this." She goes after Rafael like she's going to strangle him.

"You won't get anything if you strangle the photographer!" Rafael exclaims.

Cooper joins us and claps Owen on the shoulder. "Congratulations, you two. Shayla, he was a mess when you broke up. Practically draped himself across the bar in despair."

Owen jabs him in the ribs, and Cooper laughs.

"It was definitely a whisky night, but I got him back on track," Cooper says. "Told him I'd never let a woman like you go. He took my advice, and it all worked out."

"Is that so?" I ask Owen.

"He had nothing to do with it," Owen grumbles. "Go bug someone else with your woman advice."

Finn comes over to congratulate us. "Is Olivia here?"

Aww, he's still got a monster crush on her. "No, she couldn't make it, but she'll be at the wedding."

Finn shoves his hands in his trouser pockets. "Cool. Maybe I'll see her then."

"I'll tell her you were asking about her," I say.

"Nah. That's okay. I get that she's busy." He backs away. "Incoming."

"Yay!" Harper exclaims, rushing us both for a hug. "Welcome to the family, Shay."

Mackenzie gives me a big hug and Owen too. "We knew you two would end up together from the first moment we saw you madly in love as teens. It was just a matter of timing."

"Wish someone would've told me," Owen says.

"We didn't know," Harper says. "We hoped."

"Me too." I turn and give Owen a kiss. "I always hoped."

"Aww," Mackenzie and Harper say in unison.

Mackenzie loops her arm through mine. "Did you eat? I told Dad to be sure to have lots of vegetables for you. I know how you like to eat healthy."

"I wouldn't mind a little cake tonight," I say.

"Good. Because we've got that too," she says.

Owen and I fill our plates at the hot buffet, and people come up to congratulate us. Most of them claim they always knew we'd get back together. I'm floating in a happy bubble of love and family when Owen's aunt Hailey bursts in through the front door, out of breath.

"Oh good, I didn't miss it." She fans herself and heads toward us.

I glance at Cooper. "Did your mom run over here in those heels?"

"She's had years of practice."

Hailey joins us, wearing a formfitting navy A-line dress and matching high heels. "Things are a little chaotic across the street, but I managed to sneak away to say congratulations. Shayla, I'm so happy Owen has you. I was really getting concerned about the lack of love in his life. You know he's never gotten serious about anyone since you."

"Thanks, Aunt Hailey," Owen says. "Spill all my dirty secrets."

She pats his bicep. "That is not a dirty secret, it's sweet."

"I'm not sweet," he grumbles.

She shakes her head. "Trust me, he's as sweet as his uncle Josh. He just has a different way of showing it, but under that gruff exterior—"

"Is a good heart," I finish for her.

She smiles. "Yes. Exactly. Sorry to congratulate and run, but I have a wedding across the street in an hour, and I really should get back." She turns toward the door. "Oh no."

A bride marches in, looking pissed off. She finds Hailey and rushes over to her in a swish of tulle. Her caramel brown hair is swept into an updo. She'd look sweet with her angelic face if not for her flashing blue eyes and ferocious scowl.

She yanks the veil off her head. "He jilted me! Just up and left! And I had to find out from his ex-girlfriend, who I never wanted at the wedding anyway!"

"Did he leave with her?" Hailey asks.

"No. She was just the smug messenger."

"Oh, Rowan, I'm—" Hailey starts.

Rowan bursts into tears.

Hailey folds her into a hug. "I'm so sorry."

Rowan sniffles. "I even invited my father, who I haven't seen in three years. This is so humiliating."

Hailey pats her back. "I know. Come with me. We'll get you some water." She guides her toward the bar.

"Water's not going to cut it," Rowan says loudly.

I turn to Owen. "That's heartbreaking. I swear if that ever happened to me—"

He pulls me close. "That's never going to happen to you. You proposed to me, and there's no going back. This groom is holding you to that."

I smile and kiss him.

A waiter stops by with a tray of champagne flutes, and we each take one.

"Oh, let's do that thing where we give each other a sip," I say, wrapping my wrist around his and offering him my glass.

He copies me perfectly and offers me a sip from his glass. "To what comes next."

"A great life together."

"With the best woman in the world. No wonder I never got over you."

"Aww."

Hailey walks by, muttering to herself about irresponsible men. She finds her husband, Josh, whom she seems to be confiding the story of the ruined wedding to. He slides an arm around her waist, listening intently.

"Do you think the bride will be okay?" I ask Owen. "Maybe we should invite her to join the party."

"I doubt she's eager to join an engagement party after getting dumped on her wedding day." He looks over to the bar, where Cooper is now playing bartender and lending an ear to the jilted bride.

"She's with Cooper, the ultimate rescuer of women. She'll be fine."

I look over, still worried. Suddenly, Owen lifts me off my feet, cradled in his arms.

"Owen! What're you doing? You already carried me over the threshold to get in here."

A few people cheer, and whistles ring out.

"I had to get your attention. Time to lead off the dancing portion of the night."

I snuggle close to his chest. "I like the kissing part better."

He kisses me. "I like the sexy part." He carries me into the back room, which is empty, and proceeds to kiss the breath from me.

He cradles my cheek. "I can't wait to get you alone back home."

I smile. "Me too."

Home with Owen. It's everything I've always wanted. Even if we move around the world or have to be long distance now and then, home will always be wherever Owen is. The only man I've ever loved.

Would you like to read about Owen and Shayla's special anniversary celebration? Sign up for my newsletter for a special Bonus Epilogue! https://www.kyliegilmore.com/TKPnewsletter

Don't miss the next book in the series, *The Sexy Part*, where Cooper comes to the rescue for a jilted bride with fire in her eyes.

Cooper

One look at the jilted bride with fire in her eyes, and I'm hooked. Of course I'm going to help her get back on her feet. I have connections all over town. Soon I've found her a place to stay, a job, and friendly people to hang with, including me.

The timing's terrible for her, yet I can't stay away. But how do I convince a woman with one foot out the door to stay and give us a chance?

Rowan

So here I am, a city girl, stuck in small town Clover Park, where the wedding was supposed to take place. After being taken in by a conman, I've vowed never to fall in love again no matter how sexy, sweet, and charming a man is. Men can't be trusted.

Even if Cooper Campbell has stepped in exactly when I needed him. As soon as I get out of this massive debt my ex left me, I'm going back to my old life in the city.

Except the more I get to know Cooper, the harder he is to resist.

P.S. Did you know that Owen's parents have their own story? Check out *Hidden Hollywood*.

ALSO BY KYLIE GILMORE

The Happy Endings in Clover Park series<<2nd generation Happy Endings Book Club love!

The Kissing Part (Book 1)

The Sexy Part (Book 2)

The Sweet Part (Book 3)

The Fun Part (Book 4)

The Tempting Part (Book 5)

Happy Endings Book Club Series <<the Campbell family and a romance book club collide!

Hidden Hollywood (Book 1)

Inviting Trouble (Book 2)

So Revealing (Book 3)

Formal Arrangement (Book 4)

Bad Boy Done Wrong (Book 5)

Mess With Me (Book 6)

Resisting Fate (Book 7)

Chance of Romance (Book 8)

Wicked Flirt (Book 9)

An Inconvenient Plan (Book 10)

A Happy Endings Wedding (Book 11)

The Clover Park Series <<brothers who put family first!

The Opposite of Wild (Book 1)

Daisy Does It All (Book 2)

Bad Taste in Men (Book 3)

Kissing Santa (Book 4)

Restless Harmony (Book 5)

Not My Romeo (Book 6)

Rev Me Up (Book 7)

An Ambitious Engagement (Book 8)

Clutch Player (Book 9)

A Tempting Friendship (Book 10)

Clover Park Bride: Nico and Lily's Wedding

A Valentine's Day Gift (Book 11)

Maggie Meets Her Match (Book 12)

The Clover Park Charmers series <<sweet and sexy charmers!

Almost Over It (Book 1)

Almost Married (Book 2)

Almost Fate (Book 3)

Almost in Love (Book 4)

Almost Romance (Book 5)

Almost Hitched (Book 6)

The Rourkes Series <<swoonworthy princes and kickass princesses!

Royal Catch (Book 1)

Royal Hottie (Book 2)

Royal Darling (Book 3)

Royal Charmer (Book 4)

Royal Player (Book 5)

Royal Shark (Book 6)

Rogue Prince (Book 7)

Rogue Gentleman (Book 8)

Rogue Rascal (Book 9)

Rogue Angel (Book 10)

Rogue Devil (Book 11)

Rogue Beast (Book 12)

Unleashed Romance <<steamy romcoms with dogs!

Fetching (Book 1)

Dashing (Book 2)

Sporting (Book 3)

Toying (Book 4)

Blazing (Book 5)

Chasing (Book 6)

Daring (Book 7)

Leading (Book 8)

Racing (Book 9)

Loving (Book 10)

**Check out my website for the most up-to-date list of my books:
kyliegilmore.com/books**

ABOUT THE AUTHOR

Kylie Gilmore is the *USA Today* bestselling author of over fifty humorous contemporary romances. Her series include Happy Endings in Clover Park, Unleashed Romance, the Rourkes, the Happy Endings Book Club, Clover Park, and Clover Park Charmers. With more than three million downloads of her books, readers all over the world love escaping into her hilarious feel-good romances featuring strong bonds with family, friends, and community.

Kylie lives in New York with her family. When she's not writing, reading hot romance, or dutifully taking notes at writing conferences, you can find her happily crafting what will surely be future family heirlooms.

Sign up for Kylie's Newsletter: https://www.kyliegilmore.com/TKPnewsletter

For text alerts on Kylie's new releases, text KYLIE to the number (888) 707-3025. (US only)

For more fun stuff check out Kylie's website https://www.kyliegilmore.com.